Miss Aggie's Gone Missing

Center Point
Large Print

This Large Print Book carries the
Seal of Approval of N.A.V.H.

Miss Aggie's Gone Missing

A "Misadventure of Miss Aggie" Mystery

Frances Devine

CENTER POINT LARGE PRINT
THORNDIKE, MAINE

This Center Point Large Print edition
is published in the year 2011 by arrangement with
Barbour Publishing, Inc.

The text of this Large Print edition is unabridged.
In other aspects, this book may vary
from the original edition.
Printed in the United States of America
on permanent paper.
Set in 16-point Times New Roman type.

ISBN: 978-1-61173-093-7

Library of Congress Cataloging-in-Publication Data

Devine, Frances.
Miss Aggie's gone missing : a misadventure of Miss Aggie
mystery / Frances Devine. — Center Point large print ed.
p. cm.
ISBN 978-1-61173-093-7 (lib. binding : alk. paper)
1. Large type books. I. Title.
PS3604.E88635M57 2011
813′.6—dc22

2011003533

It's only logical that I dedicate my first mystery to my granddaughter, Amanda Guidry, who shares my love of mysteries. So, this one is for you, Mandy. I hope you enjoy it.

For all my children and grandchildren. Remember, dreams do come true and God really will give you the desires of your heart. I love you so much.

Tracey, we both know I would never have done this without your encouragement. Or was that bullying? Well, whichever it was, thank you.

Thanks to Marion and Megan of Critique Group 18; Barb, Cara, Drew and Wayne of Critique Group 25; Angie Shivers for the read-through; the ladies of Lebanon Family Church and The Hughes Center Gang who prayed for me; and very special thanks to my friend Carol Maniaci who encourages me daily. Most of all, heavenly Father, I know who holds my future. I love you.

Miss Aggie's Gone Missing

At 10:29 a.m. on a cold day in January, the Cedar Chapel Bank was robbed. At 5:41 that afternoon, Miss Georgina burst into my office at Cedar Lodge Boardinghouse, screeching like Clyde Foster's parrot, Whatzit, and flung herself into the easy chair in the corner. "Victoria!" she gasped. "Something terrible has happened!"

Figuring she meant the bank robbery, I wasn't too concerned. We'd already discussed it several times that day. However, since Miss Georgina goes into a tizzy at least three times a day, maybe this was something else. Someone had probably moved her knitting or something. I knew from past experience if she didn't calm down soon the whole household would be in an uproar. By the time I put down the mystery I'd been reading, slid my chair back, stood, and scurried over to Miss Georgina, she was sobbing hysterically.

"There, there, now," I crooned. "What in the world is the matter?"

I reached over to smooth her hair in what I thought was a comforting movement and realized in a flash I'd done the unpardonable. Somehow, I'd managed to displace the pearl comb she wore in her silver curls. I closed my eyes and waited for her pained correction of my faux pas. To my surprise, she didn't even acknowledge the cockeyed comb. Instead, Miss Georgina sniffled and grabbed my hand.

Anxiety twisted the elderly woman's face. This was more than misplaced knitting.

"I'm so worried. Aggie hasn't come home yet. She's been gone most of the day." With that, her fraught nerves gave way, and she burst into a fresh bout of sobs.

Okay. This I could handle.

"Now, now, she's been late before. I'm sure she just lost track of time and is still at the library. I'll look up the number, and we'll have her home safe and sound in no time."

As quick as the hysteria had started, Miss Georgina stopped cold and gave me an indignant scowl. All my elderly boarders felt like they could correct me at will. After all, they'd known me since I was a child and didn't care a bit that I had just turned thirty.

"Aggie never stays out past four on Tuesdays. That's the day we have our Bible study before dinner. Besides, the library closes at four thirty."

Hmmm. She did have a point. After almost a year as owner of Cedar Lodge, I should remember these little details. "Well, maybe she stopped to visit with someone."

"In this weather? It's been snowing for two hours." Once more, fear shadowed her wrinkled face.

"Miss Georgina, I'm sure Miss Aggie's fine. She'll show up any minute now."

"Maybe . . . but . . ." She leaned toward me and lowered her voice almost to a whisper. "Martin thinks the robbers took her."

A gasp from the doorway drew my attention, and I glanced up to see four heads, with hair ranging from salt-and-pepper to white as a fresh layer of snow, peering in from the hallway. Fear etched each elderly countenance, and I felt its tentacles wrapping around my own heart. Could it be true? Or was I allowing Miss Georgina's terror to affect my common sense? I forced a little laugh, which came out sounding like a hiccup.

"Now, why in the world would anyone want to kidnap Miss Aggie?"

"But Victoria, she left the house at ten fifteen this morning. What if she saw their faces?"

In the doorway, four heads nodded solemnly, and Miss Georgina wrung her plump hands.

Okay, that did it. There was only one thing to do.

"I'm sure she's fine, but I can see you're all very worried, so I'll go look for her. Just let me get my coat. Would someone tell Corky to hold dinner for a while?" I popped upstairs to my bedroom and pulled my coat from the closet. By the time I got back downstairs, the house seemed eerily quiet, with the exception of Corky, banging around in the kitchen.

"Where is everyone?" I asked.

He gave a head-jerk toward the door to the garage. I suspected Corky's attitude came as a result of his fearing his delicious meal would dry out and get cold. Or maybe he was upset because he was having to stay late. But I wasn't about to let his surliness deflect me from my purpose.

Five bundled-up figures waited by the green van, wearing a hodgepodge of expressions on their faces, from Miss Georgina's apologetic little smile to Frank Cordell's challenging glare. Miss Jane Brody stood tapping her foot, while Martin Downey's skinny frame slouched against the van door. Miss Evalina Swayne, retired schoolteacher, raised one eyebrow as though questioning if I was going to put up a fuss or not. As I glanced from one to another, a familiar surge of affection welled up in my chest. I'd known these old folks even before Grandma turned Cedar Lodge into a boardinghouse. Most of them had been close friends of Grandma and Grandpa's from the time they were young adults. And they'd remained staunch friends through the years. Sure, they sometimes bickered and fought over the silliest things, but their love and concern for one another was as solid as granite.

"Okay, then. So how about we all go?" I opened the van door, waited until they had piled in, then slid the door shut. I had a hunch this was going to be an interesting ride.

As I backed the van out of the driveway, I

realized the snow that had started falling lightly this afternoon had gotten heavier, and excitement washed over me. I'd been eagerly waiting for the first snowfall for two months. The white stuff is a rare occurrence in Texas, where I grew up, although they do get some ice now and then. This was my first winter in Missouri since inheriting the lodge, and the sight of the big flakes against the windshield made me want to sing "Jingle Bells."

Miss Georgina, however, didn't share my childlike exuberance.

"I hope it doesn't get slick before we get back."

"Georgina, calm down. We're going to be fine." At the excitement in Miss Jane's voice, I turned my head and looked. Her eyes were dancing in spite of her worry. It was all I could do not to grin. Miss Jane was always ready for adventure of any kind.

"We won't be gone that long, Miss Georgina." My words of reassurance added to Miss Jane's didn't prevent a worried sigh from escaping her lips.

She shifted her plump body and leaned her head back on the seat. "I hope you're right."

My heart went out to her as her shaking hand adjusted the seat belt. Only her love and concern for Miss Aggie could have pulled her from the house during inclement weather. I gave her a mental thumbs-up at the sacrifice.

I drove the short block to High Street, on past the

town square to Main, and turned left toward the library. The downtown district was all but deserted except for a few tired shop clerks and court employees trudging to their cars through the fresh mounds of snow. I cautiously drove the three blocks past the library to the end of Main with no sign of Miss Aggie. Making a slow U-turn, I headed back and drove the five blocks to Miller's Supermarket. I pulled into the parking lot with a sigh of relief. I wasn't used to driving in snow, and despite my assurances to Miss Georgina, it was making me a tad nervous. The parking lot boasted a few scattered cars, but Miss Aggie's wasn't among them.

"Let's stop here and see if maybe Miss Aggie had a craving for sweets. You know how she likes her piece of chocolate after dinner. I remember her saying last night she'd finished her last one."

"If Aggie wanted sweets all she had to do was ask, and I would have brought her some chocolate back from my place." Frank Cordell spoke up from the backseat. Frank's son had inherited the family candy store when Frank retired eighteen years ago. Under Junior's loving hand, the business had exploded into a successful franchise with shops all over Missouri, Kansas, and Oklahoma. But Frank's heart still belonged to the first store he opened and named after his sweetheart and wife, Betty. Junior had left BETTY'S painted in the original store window, but all other shops were simply Cordell's Candy. I should have known better than to suggest

Miss Aggie would dare buy candy anywhere else.

"Well, maybe someone in here has seen her."

"That's right," Miss Georgina said, her sweet voice barely audible. "Aggie did tell me she needed some denture cream." She gave me a hopeful and watery look. "Do you think maybe she stopped off here?"

I reached out and gave her an encouraging pat. "I'll find out."

"I don't think Miz Brown would be going shopping this time of night." Martin Downey's mournful voice drowned out the little hopeful chirps emitting from the ladies.

"Let's go look anyway, Mr. Downey. You know women sometimes get strange and sudden impulses." I tried to sound cheerful, but as I hurried into the store, trailed by all five of the elderly friends, a little niggling bit of worry wormed its way into my head. It was getting darker by the minute, and the snow was coming down harder. Miss Aggie should have been in her sweet-smelling bedroom, putting the finishing touches on her unusual, still-black hair before dinner. This wasn't like her at all. A quick search through the grocery store failed to turn up any sign of the missing woman, and the employees denied seeing Miss Aggie at all that day.

"Maybe she's at home, wondering where we all are." I tried to sound hopeful and almost managed to convince myself, as we piled back into the van.

"Hhmph." Only Miss Evalina Swayne could harrumph in quite that way. "Hhmph," she repeated. "I knew this was nothing but a wild goose chase. Aggie is probably at the lodge watching *Wheel of Fortune* right this minute and wondering where we all are. We're going to look mighty foolish when she finds out what we've been up to."

I hoped she was right. Prayed so.

After driving up and down some of the side streets, just in case, I headed back toward home.

We pulled up in front of the old stone lodge and got out. Miss Georgina stumbled as she stepped out of the car, and I reached out quickly and took her arm.

"Careful. Don't slip on the snow, now." She steadied herself, and I hurried up to the porch and into the foyer, while the others followed cautiously up the slick steps. We stopped in our tracks as Corky came out of the kitchen. The foyer was dark, but light from the porch shone into the room and cast a strange glow onto the cook's face, giving him a sinister look. *Really, Victoria,* I thought, *pull yourself together.* Reason took over and I shook off the illusion. The questioning look on Corky's face told it all. But I had to ask. "Is she here?"

He shook his head.

A wail issued from Miss Georgina's lips as she swayed. I grabbed her, and she peered up at me, tears flooding her faded blue eyes.

"Victoria, I just know something's happened to Aggie."

• • •

Sheriff Turner's questions were starting to get on my nerves. You'd think he suspected us of having something to do with Miss Aggie's disappearance. Couldn't he see how worried everyone was?

We'd sat here in the great room for nearly an hour going over and over the same things. The fire in the fireplace was roaring, thanks to an overzealous Corky, and I was starting to perspire. At first the sheriff had suspected that Miss Aggie had taken off on one of her little trips. She'd done this before without telling anyone where she was going. But after searching her room and finding all her clothing and personal items there, he'd finally begun to take us seriously. But why was he dawdling so? Didn't he know time was wasting? What if Miss Aggie had fallen somewhere and broken a hip or something? Or maybe even . . . well, what if she really had been kidnapped? I was about ready to take the twirling billy club from his hand and throw it into the fire when he cleared his throat and nodded his head.

"So, allegedly, Miss Aggie left the house at ten fifteen to go to the library. She was wearing a black-and-white pantsuit and drove away in a light blue 1993 Taurus GL. Is that right?"

"For crying out loud, Bob. You know what Aggie drives as well as we do," Frank sputtered.

The sheriff eyed Frank then continued, "And

none of you've seen her since she drove off down the street."

Five heads, including Frank's, nodded solemnly for the umpteenth time, and I could feel mine starting to bob as well.

"Aggie always goes to the library in the morning." Miss Georgina's voice quivered. "She's usually home by lunchtime, but sometimes she goes to the senior center for lunch. Sometimes we all do. Not that their lunches are much good, but it's nice to visit with our friends there."

"And play bingo," Martin piped up, like maybe this bit of information might be helpful to the case. I understood his frustration. The need to do *something.*

"Well, I most certainly do not play bingo." Miss Evalina spoke emphatically, all the while frowning at Martin. "Gambling is gambling no matter what you call it. I don't care if they are just playing for pies and donuts." She looked at Sheriff Turner and nodded her head as if that settled it.

"Tsk tsk tsk." I wasn't sure what the sound coming from Frank's tongue meant, but he cut his gaze to Miss Evalina. She jerked her head around, and as their eyes met, her face took on a decidedly pinkish hue. I felt my curiosity rising.

Sheriff Turner turned to his deputy, Tom Lewis, who stood leaning against the door, eating one of Corky's apple turnovers. There were plenty left, since none of us had felt like eating dinner.

"Tom, why don't you head on over to the Chancys' and ask Louise if Aggie ever made it to the library? I think that's the first step. Then meet me at the office. I'll call around and see if anyone in town has seen her."

"Won't do no good," Martin piped up. "Told you. We've called everyone."

The sheriff stood and threw an annoyed glance in Martin's direction. "Well, maybe you missed someone, Martin. Or maybe someone has thought of something since then."

He turned to me. "If she shows up or if anyone thinks of anything else, you be sure to call me."

"I will, Sheriff. And you'll call us if you find out anything, won't you?"

He nodded slightly, cleared his throat, and left. I wasn't sure if that nod was a commitment or not.

I looked around at the others. Confusion seemed to be the expression on every face, to one degree or another, except for Miss Evalina, who peered at me through squinted eyes. I wondered what was getting ready to proceed from her lips. She didn't make me wonder for long.

"Well, missy, what do you intend to do?" She sat with her foot tapping the floor and her thin lips sternly pressed together as she waited for my answer. Why did I always feel like a child in her presence?

"What do you mean? We just have to wait for the sheriff to find Miss Aggie."

A look of exasperation crossed her face. And something else. Disappointment?

"Your grandmother would have done something more."

Warmth flooded my cheeks, and a knot formed in my stomach. This was the first time any of them had compared me to Grandma.

"But, Miss Evalina, what could Grandma have possibly done?"

"I don't know. But she would have done something."

With that, she stood, walked stiffly from the room, and ascended the stairs.

I glanced helplessly at the other four but didn't get any comfort from the looks on their faces. Apparently they agreed with Miss Evalina, albeit silently.

The phone shrilled. We all jumped, and Miss Georgina screamed, her hand to her heart, then she gave an embarrassed little laugh. I shook my head at our nerves and picked up the receiver. "Good evening. Cedar Lodge."

"Vickie? It's Ben Grant."

As if I wouldn't know that voice anywhere.

"Hi, Benjamin. What can I do for you?"

"I've heard a rumor that Aggie Brown has disappeared. I'd like to stop by and get the details if that's okay."

Benjamin in my house? On my turf? Not a chance. "Why?"

"Why? I do run a newspaper, Vickie." Was that sarcasm? Yes, that was definitely sarcasm.

"I'm aware of that, Ben," I snapped. "But there's very little to tell. Miss Aggie left for the library at ten fifteen this morning and isn't home yet. I'm sure there's a perfectly logical explanation. So . . . no news story here. Sorry."

"Hmm . . . I was told it might be related to the bank robbery. Sorry I bothered you. I hope she turns up safe and sound."

"Thanks. I'm sure she will. Good-bye."

I hung up the receiver and exhaled. Did the whole town know about Miss Aggie? And did everyone think she had been kidnapped? I shivered and glanced over at the group huddled on the sofas around the fireplace, where the fire had finally burned down to a nice crackling flame. I needed to do something. But what? We'd called all over town. We'd told the sheriff. What else could I do?

I sat back down on the wing chair near the others. They looked at me expectantly.

"You should have let Ben come over, Victoria," Miss Jane said.

Martin straightened up. "She's right. We need some help here. Why'd you tell him not to come?"

"What in the world do you think Benjamin Grant can do? He's not a detective."

"But, Victoria . . . ," Miss Georgina said. "Everyone knows newspaper men solve crimes. They always do in the movies."

Miss Jane let out a sigh of exasperation. "The movies! Really!"

Frank snorted. "It has nothing to do with movies. Benjamin's smart as a whip. Great mind on that boy. And in his business, I'm sure he's seen a lot of missing person cases."

Maybe they were right. Everyone kept telling me Ben had "grown up into a fine young man," but all I could think of were incidents of terrorism when we were kids. With my chihuahua, Sparky, as the victim. And Ben as the terrorist. Still . . . this wasn't about me. It was about finding Miss Aggie. And if there was the slightest chance he could help . . .

I got up and headed for the phone.

The corner fireplace in the small parlor needed another log, but none of us bothered. Since Benjamin had arrived two hours earlier, we'd filled him in on everything we could think of concerning the day's happenings. He'd asked a few questions about Miss Aggie's daily habits, taking notes as we talked. Then, at Frank Cordell's insistence, Benjamin compared Aggie's disappearance with some of the missing person cases he'd covered in St. Louis. I, for one, was getting depressed. Furthermore, Miss Georgina was looking a little green.

"Benjamin." Miss Evalina's voice exploded. "What exactly does any of this have to do with Aggie? If you have nothing constructive to say, why did you bother to come?"

I stared at the ever-so-proper retired schoolteacher. This wasn't like her at all. Benjamin seemed a little bit miffed, and who could blame him? After all, Mr. Cordell had requested the stories.

"Actually, Miss Evalina, I just came to get some details for the newspaper. I certainly don't pretend to be a detective. I wish I could help, but . . ."

His voice trailed off, and he tossed a helpless look in my direction.

"That's true," I said, coming to his rescue. "When he called he said he needed information for the paper."

"Eva, what's got into you?" Frank snapped. "Why are you being so dad-blamed negative? Who knows if some of these other cases might tickle our memories about something important?"

Miss Evalina's face flamed. "What do you know about anything, Frank Cordell? You're nothing but a big-mouth and a show-off."

An embarrassed silence pervaded the room. Miss Georgina and Miss Jane gave each other side glances and shook their heads. Miss Evalina had the grace to blush as she pointedly turned her back on Mr. Cordell. Whatever the conflict was between those two, it was getting worse.

Benjamin stood up. "I need to go. If there's anything at all I can do, I'll be glad to help."

Maybe he has *changed,* I thought, tossing him a smile. "I know, and we appreciate it. But perhaps we'll just have to let the sheriff take care of this."

I cringed as Miss Evalina emitted a loud huff. I had no idea what she expected me to do, but it was clear she expected something.

I walked Benjamin to the door, and we stepped onto the wide porch. A heavy veil of snow continued to fall, and lights from the house and street flickered on the snow-covered ground. I shivered.

What if Miss Aggie were out in this weather? I closed my eyes and whispered, "Father, please watch over her. We don't know where she is, but You do."

I opened my eyes to find Benjamin looking at me strangely, his eyes intense and questioning.

"You really think that's going to help?"

"What? Prayer?"

"Yeah. You don't really believe that stuff, do you?"

"Of course I believe it. Don't you?"

"I dunno. Seems if there's anyone up there, He isn't paying much attention to us poor slobs down here."

Irritation rose up in me. "Cut it out, Benjamin," I snapped. "That's not a bit funny."

I frowned at him, expecting him to burst out laughing, but to my surprise he remained silent. My stomach knotted. Benjamin had been raised in a Christian home the same as I had. Maybe this was simply another attempt by him to get under my skin.

"You didn't mean that, did you?" I asked.

He rubbed his hand over the dark stubble on his chin and chuckled in a strangled voice. "Has He ever really done anything to prove He's up there and cares about you?" His forehead wrinkled, and I drew in a sharp breath at the pain in his eyes.

My heart sped up. Living here in Cedar Chapel,

I hadn't found it necessary to defend my faith in a long time. I licked my lips and offered up a silent prayer.

"He proves it every day, Benjamin. I couldn't have made it through Grandma's death without Him." *And the heartbreak of a broken relationship. The agony of discovering that my fiancé was unfaithful.* I shoved the thought quickly away. "And running this place would be impossible without His help. I know He's there, and I know He cares about me."

Benjamin's mouth quirked up in a sardonic smile. "Well, I wouldn't want to burst your little bubble. Maybe you're right. G'night, Vickie." Whistling, he walked to his car and got in. Throwing me a two-fingered salute, he drove off down the street.

"Good night, Benjamin," I whispered.

When I got back inside, Miss Evalina was marching up the stairs, followed by the rest of the troop. I turned off the lights and headed upstairs, too, still disturbed by Benjamin's remarks.

I'd just finished my shower and settled in for my evening devotions when someone tapped on the door. A resident probably needed clean towels or something, I thought. After slipping into my robe, I opened the door. Miss Evalina stood there with a determined look on her face.

"I think we should look through Aggie's room," she said.

The sheriff had told us in no uncertain terms to stay out of there. And she knew that. “Miss Evalina, you know Sheriff Turner and Deputy Lewis searched the room earlier.” I tried to sound as gentle as possible. She was obviously more worried than I’d realized.

“I know it, but . . .” The wrinkles on her forehead deepened and multiplied. “It’s just Aggie’s room. We’ve been in there hundreds of times. And maybe we’ll find something that Bob and Tom missed. Because we know Aggie better. You know?” Her bottom lip quivered, and she quickly tightened it into a straight line.

She did have a point. I stood for a moment, waffling back and forth, then shook my head. “Can’t do it, Miss Evalina. Sorry. We’ll have to let the sheriff handle it.”

I placed my hand on her shoulder. “I think I’ll have some tea. Would you like a cup?”

She shook her head absently as I turned off my light and stepped into the hall. We walked quietly down the carpeted hallway toward her bedroom. As we passed Miss Aggie’s room, I stopped short. A crack of light filtered through from beneath the door. Glancing over my shoulder, I motioned Miss Evalina back and carefully turned the doorknob. A familiar shriek bounced off our ears, and the light went out.

“It’s no use, ladies. Turn the light back on,” I said firmly and then tightened my lips to keep from smiling as the dim hallway light revealed two shadows huddled on the floor.

There was a moment of silence then a sigh followed by scurrying. Light flooded the room, revealing Miss Jane and Miss Georgina standing by Miss Aggie's four-poster bed.

"Victoria, please don't be angry," Miss Georgina's tiny voice pleaded as she twisted the hanky in her hands.

"Oh, she's not mad. Are you?" Miss Jane threw me one of her fake Southern belle smiles, and I couldn't keep from grinning as she continued. "I mean, you and Evalina had the same idea, didn't you?"

I couldn't very well deny that. "Well, yes we did, but we'd decided against it. You do know this is illegal, don't you?" At the look of fear on Miss Georgina's face, I relented. "But no, I'm not angry. Have you found anything?"

"Not yet. I was just about to peek into Aggie's old diary." She held up a small black leather book.

"Oh no you don't, Jane Brody." Miss Evalina held out her hand and fluttered her fingers for the book. Miss Jane hesitated and then, with a pout and a defiant look, handed the book to me.

"Here. You look through it and see if you can find any clues." She cast a triumphant look at Evalina.

"Thanks, but I think going through her diary might be a little extreme." I placed the worn little book on the bedside table.

Miss Aggie's room was neat as a pin. The lace-trimmed coverlet and shams were without wrinkle and the dresser uncluttered, with her brush and mirror neatly arranged. The small nightstand held only a small lamp and a magazine advertising elegant inns.

"Okay, we're already in here so we might as well look around. Maybe we can find something that would help Miss Aggie. Let's each take a section of the room and make sure we search carefully. If anything at all looks out of place or seems strange, examine it closely." I started with Miss Aggie's closet. Her clothing hung on the rack, dresses and skirts at one end, jackets and blouses at the other. A few boxes were stacked neatly on the shelf above, and shoes were lined up in a row on the closet floor. The boxes overflowed with memorabilia from years past. A scent of old paper and dried flowers wafted from them, creating a slight musty smell in the closet. I removed a few letters tied with faded blue ribbon then replaced them. They might be entertaining, but I doubted a stack of old letters would yield any clues to Miss Aggie's whereabouts. Next, I turned to the antique walnut desk and started searching through the top drawer, though my stomach clenched at the intrusion.

"Has anyone come across a diamond choker necklace or a heart-shaped diamond ring?"

I looked up to see Miss Evalina holding a cherry wood jewelry box.

"I didn't know she had anything like that. I don't remember seeing her wear them," I said.

"She hasn't in years. Her father gave her the necklace when she turned eighteen and . . ." She hesitated then went on, so quietly I could barely make out the words. "Someone else gave her the ring."

"Were the pieces very expensive, or were the diamonds just chips?"

"The ring was a full carat, specially cut into a heart shape, and the choker was worth thousands of dollars even back then. I can only imagine its value now." Miss Evalina's face drained of color. "Does anyone know if she was wearing them this morning?"

"Oh no, I'm sure she wasn't," said Miss Georgina. "She had on the locket she always wears."

"Let me see if they're in the desk," I said. "I can't imagine why they would be, but I'd better check." A thorough search failed to turn up the missing diamonds. I held up my hands in defeat. "Wouldn't she keep them in a vault at the bank?" I questioned.

Miss Evalina shook her head. "I just saw them last week. She showed them off to *me* every chance she got." She bit her lip and grew silent. Apparently the words had slipped out unintentionally.

Hmmm. That didn't sound like Miss Aggie to me. But maybe Miss Evalina knew something I didn't. After all, they'd been friends all their lives.

"We'll have to report this to the sheriff in the morning. In the meantime, ladies, I think we've done about all we can."

After a restless night, I called the sheriff and reported the missing jewels. Knowing I deserved it, I listened silently as he raked me over the coals for searching the room.

"Sorry, Sheriff. Of course you're right." Sometimes meekness is the best policy.

While eating breakfast, my mind kept returning to the diary and letters. Would it hurt to take a little peek just to make sure? I shook my head. Couldn't do it. As old as they were, I didn't expect to find anything relevant in them anyway.

I had a few errands to attend to, and as I drove around the icy square to find a parking place, I couldn't help wondering how everything could look so normal when, in fact, our lives had been severely shaken. I took care of the errands and some business matters and then decided to go talk to Louise Chancy, the town librarian.

The library was quiet as a grave, as usual, and smelled about as dusty. I shuddered at the morbid thought and went looking for Louise. I found her in the children's section, shelving books.

As I approached, she looked up from her stool then sneezed.

"Good morning, Mrs. Chancy. Could we talk for a few minutes?"

She squinted at me. It looked like she'd forgotten her glasses again. "Oh. Victoria. Just give me a minute to get the rest of this row done."

A familiar title caught my eye, and I reached down into the tub and picked up a book. "I see Nancy Drew is still around."

"Yes, but I hardly recognize her." The tiny woman nodded her head and gave a nervous twitter. "When I was a girl, she was driving a roadster. Times have certainly changed."

I chuckled, although I had no idea what a roadster was. I handed her the book and she slid it into its place on the shelf then struggled to her feet, obviously winded. They really needed to get her an assistant. Someone younger to do shelving and so forth. Maybe I should volunteer a couple of days a week.

"Let's go to the front, Victoria, and I'll get us some coffee."

I followed her to the little alcove off the front lobby and waited in one of the wingback chairs until she brought two hot, steaming mugs and set them on a small table. She leaned back in her chair and gave a sigh of relief.

"Sorry. I was awake most of the night. Too much excitement, I guess. Have you heard anything from Aggie yet?"

"No, we haven't heard a word. Are you sure she didn't make it here at all yesterday? Is there any chance she came in but you didn't see her?"

She shook her head. "I'm sorry. Like I told Sheriff Turner, she didn't come in at all. I was at the desk all morning, except when I met Lillian Baker for lunch. And the library was locked up tight then."

Frustration overwhelmed me. An elderly lady couldn't just drop out of existence without any sign at all, could she? Someone had to have seen something. "She hasn't done or said anything out of the ordinary lately?" I hated to persist, but I wasn't leaving until I was sure there were no leads here.

She shook her head again. "No. Everything was the same . . ." She hesitated, and doubt flashed across her face.

"What? Have you thought of something?" I heard my voice rising and softened my tone. "Mrs. Chancy, if there is anything at all. Even if you don't think it's important, please tell me."

"Well, there is something. But . . . it's probably nothing at all, and I don't think I'm supposed to reveal information about the patrons."

"But Miss Aggie isn't just a patron, she's your friend." I gazed at her, and seeing her uncertainty, I pleaded, "Please, Mrs. Chancy."

Her eyes widened. Then she blurted, "She's been getting on that Internet, every single day. Staying on there all morning."

"The Internet?" I tried to wrap the thought around my brain. Miss Aggie couldn't even use the microwave without help. "Miss Aggie was getting on the Internet? Are you sure?"

She nodded vigorously. "I couldn't believe it either. For most of last week she was on that computer all morning and sometimes in the afternoon, too. I asked her what in the world she was doing, but she flat out told me to mind my own business."

"Did you ever find out what she was up to?"

"After her telling me off like that? No, ma'am. I minded my own business just like she said." Suddenly her face crumpled and her voice broke. "I guess I shouldn't be mad at her anymore. I just wish she were back here safe and sound."

I murmured a few words of comfort and thanked her for her help. Promising to keep in touch, I left and headed for the courthouse. This was a piece of information Sheriff Turner needed to know. As I rushed into the sheriff's department, Tom looked up from the counter.

"Tom, is the sheriff in?" I asked.

"Yep."

"Well, I need to see him. Right now."

"Nope." He scratched his chin and leaned back in his chair.

"What do you mean 'nope'? You just said he's in."

"Yep, but you can't see him. He doesn't want to be disturbed."

"Listen, Tom. I have to see him. Please tell him I'm here." I leaned over the counter and gave him an imploring look.

"No, ma'am. He's busy, and I'm not about to bother him."

Dropping the supplicant act, I pushed back from the counter and put both hands on my hips. After all, hadn't I been emulating the great Agatha Christie's feisty heroines since I was sixteen? I mustered up the most intimidating glare I could manage. "Look, bud. I have some important information about Miss Aggie's disappearance. If you don't tell him I'm here, I'm going to walk in there unannounced. Then you'll really get in trouble."

Tom tossed me a dirty look, but to my surprise he got up and headed back to the sheriff's office. He returned shortly and motioned me toward the other room.

When I walked into the cluttered office, Sheriff Turner shook the hand I offered and told me to take a seat. Tom walked over to a small table across the room and started sorting through papers, taking his time, with one ear cocked in our direction.

I leaned forward. "Sheriff, I just found out that Miss Aggie has been using the library computers to get on the Internet."

He just sat and looked at me as if waiting for more. "And your point is?"

"Well, don't you think it's a little strange that an elderly woman should suddenly start surfing the Web? Her main hobbies are quilting and leading a senior ladies' Bible study."

"What exactly are you trying to say, Victoria? Just get to the point, please."

I blew a strand of hair out of my eyes before speaking. "What if Miss Aggie is a victim of an Internet scam artist? Or maybe something worse. Like a sexual predator." I sat back in the chair. There. Let's see what he'd say about that!

Strangled laughter came from across the room and Tom doubled over, pounding his knee. As though they were hooked up to the same wire, both men howled with laughter.

I stood, pulled myself up as tall as my five feet four inches would allow, and glared at them both.

"Excuse me, but I don't see anything funny about Miss Aggie being in the hands of a killer . . . or worse."

The sheriff sobered and looked at me sternly. "Now you listen here, Victoria Storm. That's the most ridiculous idea I've ever heard. Miss Aggie was more than likely just doing some online shopping or playing solitaire on the Web. You just get home and leave this case to me and my department and keep your nose out of it." He leaned forward and steepled his hands on the scarred desk. "I probably shouldn't tell you this, but I'm pretty sure the bank robbers made off with Miss Aggie."

I leaned forward. "Oh, then you do have some information? Someone saw something? Have you found her car?" Eagerly, I waited for the first piece of real information since Miss Aggie's disappearance.

"Well, no, it's just a matter of deduction. You know."

My mouth flew open, and I stared in disbelief. "You mean it's just your theory."

"Now listen here, Miss Smarty. You just go home and keep your nose out of this before you go and get yourself hurt. You're as cantankerous as your grandma was."

"I'm leaving, Sheriff, but you haven't heard the last of this." I stomped out of the office, out the door, and drove home. As cantankerous as Grandma, huh? Well, he hadn't seen anything yet. Because Miss Evalina was right. Grandma *would* have done something. And the sheriff wasn't the only one around Cedar Chapel to say I was just like her.

Westminster chimes reverberated through the great room, bounced off the walls and ceilings, and pounded against my brain, sinister, as though heralding some imminent doom. Taking a deep breath, I laughed, and the sound, though feeble, seemed to echo from the corners of the room. I really had to pull myself together. Those chimes had announced the hours at Cedar Lodge for as long as I could remember, comforting and familiar. Still, today was different. Felt different. Looked different. Since I'd talked to Mrs. Chancy.

I stood and crossed the room to the grandfather clock standing tall and stately against the far wall, just as it had stood for more than a hundred years. Nothing sinister here. It continued its familiar count until it reached twelve. Straightening my shoulders, I headed for the dining room. Everyone would be gathered there by now, seated at the enormous, antique oak table, waiting for me. I wasn't sure how much to tell them about the latest bit of information. But they weren't children. And I'd promised I wouldn't keep anything from them.

"It's about time you got here, missy. If there's one thing I hate and abominate it's cold meatloaf."

Apparently Miss Evalina was still mad at me. She knew very well Corky's meatloaf would be served hot and delicious, straight from the small steam table in the kitchen.

Martin asked the blessing, and we ate our lunch amid silent glares from Miss Evalina and unsuccessful attempts by Miss Jane and Miss Georgina to carry on a normal conversation.

Finally, when everyone had eaten their fill, I spoke up. "Would you mind coming into the parlor? I need to discuss something with all of you."

Murmurs of assent rose from around the table, and within a few minutes everyone was seated in their favorite chairs in the parlor.

I walked across the room to the corner fireplace, stirred the burning embers, and added a small log.

"Well, get on with it, Victoria," Miss Evalina snapped.

"Now, Evalina, there's no sense in being rude to Victoria just because you're in one of your moods."

"What do you mean, moods? I'll have you know, Frank Cordell, I do not have moods."

Oh no. Were these two ever going to get over whatever was causing this bickering? They'd been at each other for two days now. But I wasn't about to get in the middle of their verbal barbs. The last time I tried that, they'd let me have it. I straightened up but stayed by the fireplace where I could see them all.

"I want to ask you something," I said.

Five faces turned to me inquisitively.

"Did Miss Aggie ever mention to any of you that she was using the computers at the library? Particularly the Internet?"

Five heads shook in unison.

"Aggie? Are you kidding? She can't even turn on the TV." Martin chuckled.

"Where'd you get a tomfool idea like that?" Frank asked.

"Mrs. Chancy told me," I said.

"Ha. I knew Aggie wasn't as quiet and strait-laced as she pretended. I'll bet she's been gambling on there." Martin's grin turned quickly to a scowl at the indignant looks that assaulted him.

I glanced at Miss Evalina, the only one who hadn't said anything. The color had drained from her face, and she looked strained as she stared into my eyes.

"Victoria," she whispered. "What are you thinking?"

"I don't know, Miss Evalina. It's just strange that Miss Aggie, of all people, would start surfing the Web."

"Yes. And even more strange that she didn't mention it."

"Oh, no. You don't think . . ." Miss Georgina stopped, at a loss for words.

Understanding dawned upon the longtime friends.

"What if she told someone about her money and they spirited her away somewhere to try to get it?" Frank exploded.

"Oh dear." Miss Georgina looked as though she'd faint any moment. She took out a small lace-trimmed hanky and fanned herself.

"Huh?" I glanced around at them in surprise. "What money? I never heard anything about any money."

Miss Jane sighed. "Oh yes, she has money. A lot of it. She's afraid to let anyone know. Because . . . well, she's just so paranoid. I can't imagine her telling anyone."

"We're probably the only folks in Cedar Chapel who've known her long enough to know the story," Frank said.

"What story? Please, I'm trying to figure this out. You need to tell me all you know."

"You tell her, Eva."

Miss Evalina started and glanced quickly at Mr. Cordell. She blushed and bit her lip. Then she looked at me and nodded.

"Well, as you know, Aggie was a Pennington. Her father was very wealthy. No one is really sure where he got his money. Some say gold mines in California, others that he was mixed up in something shady. There were those who insisted he'd entertained Frank James on occasion. But all that's just hearsay. For all I know, he inherited it. But I do know he invested wisely and held interests in businesses of one sort or another all over the

United States. He settled here and built a mansion such as no one in these parts had ever seen. It stands on a hill, up near Rhodes Springs."

"You never saw such a house," Miss Georgina put in. "It was like a castle. I mean, we weren't poor, but I'd never seen such opulence in my life."

"Yes, they even had solid gold water spigots," Martin declared.

Miss Evalina cleared her throat and waited. When no one else said anything, she continued. "Yes, well, I don't recall ever seeing gold water spigots, but nevertheless, it was quite a showplace. That was somewhere early in the 1900s. Mr. Pennington brought his young bride here in 1907. They had two children. Forrest was born around 1910, but Agatha didn't come along until 1927, the same year I was born. Forrest wasn't around much when we were growing up. First, he was away at school, then in some sort of textile business in New York City owned by his mother's family. Everyone assumed he'd eventually inherit most of his father's estate."

"But they were wrong," Frank said. "Pennington practically disinherited him."

"Are you going to let me tell this, Frank?" Miss Evalina huffed.

"Well, get on with it then. She don't need to know every little detail."

"It's okay, Mr. Cordell. I want to hear it all." I smiled at him, and he nodded and leaned back against the straight chair he'd chosen.

The doorbell rang. Exasperated, I turned to get up and saw Corky step away from the parlor door. Puzzled, I watched him as he went to open the door. What had he been doing? Listening?

Benjamin appeared in the doorway, and Corky headed back down the hall toward the kitchen.

"Hi. I was just on the block and thought I'd stop by and check on Miss Aggie. Any news about her yet?"

"Yeah, she's more than likely the victim of some Internet crook," Martin said

"Mr. Downey, we don't know that."

Benjamin threw me a questioning look.

"Mrs. Chancy told me Miss Aggie's been spending a lot of time on the Internet at the library."

He raised his brows, and suddenly I realized my statement didn't really sound so earth-shattering. Was I blowing this thing way out of proportion?

Mr. Cordell came to my rescue. "For Aggie to get on the Internet is like you or me building a shuttle and blasting off into space."

Benjamin grinned. "Oh, come on now. Even my grandmother surfs the Web. She's done a lot of trading and has sold most of her Depression glass on eBay." He laid his coat on the arm of the other wing chair and sat down. "You don't mind if I join you, do you?"

This time his grin was tossed in my direction and his eyes crinkled. I wondered why I'd never noticed how deep blue his eyes were. I didn't even remember them *being* blue. Oh, yeah. Now I remembered. Taunting, malicious blue eyes. I drew myself up and frowned at him.

He raised his eyebrows. “What?”

“Nothing.” I decided to ignore the puzzled look on his face.

“Eva was just telling Victoria about Aggie’s family,” said Miss Jane.

“Oh, yeah? She was a Pennington. Everyone knows that.”

I glanced at Miss Evalina, who looked a little bit uncertain. I could understand. After all, Benjamin did run the newspaper.

Finally, she said, “Well, Benjamin, I’ve never known you to break a confidence. And maybe you need to know everything, in order to help us get to the bottom of this. Yes, everyone knows Aggie’s father was Jason Pennington. But not everyone knows she still has a great deal of her inheritance. In fact, she’s very wealthy.”

Benjamin gave a little whistle.

“Interesting family. I know a little bit about their background. It’s still uncertain where Pennington got his money.”

“Miss Evalina, would you please continue?” I asked.

She sighed and sagged into her chair, closing her eyes for a moment. Summoning strength, she continued. “To make a long story short, Forrest took up with a dancer in some musical comedy. When he wouldn’t give her up, his father would have nothing more to do with him. I suppose Mr. Pennington had a change of heart before he died, because he did leave Forrest nearly half his holdings. Of course, by then the family fortune wasn't as large, due to some bad investments during and right after World War II, but there were still millions. But I need to get on with Aggie's part of the story." She threw a glance at Frank then licked her lips before she continued.

"Aggie was always rather flighty. Her parents spoiled her rotten, and she thought she should have anything she took a whim for." Her voice trembled, and she looked down at her hands for a moment. Clearing her throat once more, she went on. "But the day came when her whim went crosswise to her father's wishes. She wanted a young man who was not on their social or financial level. In fact, he was the son of a country doctor, a very nice man, but he barely made ends meet. Aggie threw tantrum after tantrum, but her father was adamant. For the first time in her life, he wouldn't give in.

"Not only would he not give in, but he declared she was not sound enough of mind to make her own choices or handle her inheritance. He didn't strip her of it, but his will stated she could only have access to an allowance, barely enough to live on really, until she married a man of certain financial means. Years later, her attorneys managed to get the will overturned, and she did receive her inheritance.

"A couple of years after receiving it, she married a man who turned out to be after her inheritance, just as her father had feared. He managed to go through a large amount of money before someone killed him in a brawl. She got off a lot easier than she could have. But by then, she was so afraid of fortune hunters that she became, as Jane said, quite paranoid. She closed up the house and lived a very modest life in a cottage out by the lake for years. After a while, people assumed she'd lost all her wealth. Then, when Caroline turned Cedar Lodge into a boardinghouse, she moved in here."

Ever a romantic, I asked the question that roiled in my mind. "Whatever happened to the young man who caused the stir between Aggie and her father? Is he still around these parts?"

Silence met my question. Miss Georgina and Miss Jane darted glances at one another. Martin looked up at the ceiling. Frank and Miss Evalina looked into each other's eyes.

She tore her gaze from his and looked down at her hands, clenched around a knotted-up hankie in her lap. "I'm not at liberty to divulge that information."

Frank pulled his glance away from Miss Evalina and looked at me. "Well, I am," he said. "It was me."

"Coffee anyone?" Corky stood in the doorway, a welcome relief from the embarrassment that had saturated the room since Frank made his declaration. A declaration that apparently came as no surprise except to Benjamin and me. After powder room breaks, we settled down with our coffee.

I was disappointed. Miss Aggie's story, while interesting, seemed to hold no bearing on her disappearance.

"What do you plan to do about the Internet thing, Victoria?" Miss Jane asked.

"Isn't there some way we could find out what she was up to?" Miss Evalina asked.

Now there was an idea. Why hadn't I thought of it? I turned to Benjamin. "That is possible, isn't it?"

"Yeah, but I doubt the library would agree without a go-ahead from the authorities."

"That's no good. They laughed in my face."

"Well, maybe we could convince Louise," Miss Jane said. "We have to at least try."

"What good's that going to do?" Martin's mouth twisted as he spoke. "Louise won't know anything about hacking into a computer."

I glanced around at the others then stood. "Well, it's worth a try, anyway. I'm going back to the library. Pray I can convince her."

"Pray? I can do that in the van. I'm going with you." Frank seemed pretty determined, so I knew better than to argue.

"We'll all go." Miss Evalina rose from her chair and the rest followed suit. I groaned inwardly. Oh, well. Power in numbers. Poor Mrs. Chancy. She didn't stand a chance.

"If you don't mind, Vickie, I think I'll go along for the ride." Benjamin bowed and smirked. I glared but didn't answer. Let him come along if he wanted to.

We drove to the library and went in, drawing curious glances from the few people sitting around at the tables and browsing among the shelves.

Mrs. Chancy sat behind the checkout counter.

"Louise," Miss Jane called out loudly.

Martin grabbed her arm. "Be quiet, Jane," he whispered.

Mrs. Chancy looked up, startled, and said, "Shhh."

Miss Jane nodded, jerking her arm away from Martin.

"Mrs. Chancy," I whispered. "May we talk to you in private?"

"But . . . I can't leave the desk when there are people in the library. Can't it wait? I'll be closing in a half hour."

We sat at a table in the back of the library and browsed through magazines. I had no idea what I was reading, and I doubted the others did either. The continual stress and worry of the last couple of days was wearing me down. I could only imagine how it affected these precious older people.

I glanced up to find Benjamin watching me.

"What?"

"Shh." He put his finger to his lips and grinned.

At precisely 4:03, Mrs. Chancy appeared at our table.

"Now, what do you want to talk to me about?" She listened with obvious anxiety as I explained about the files.

"No, absolutely not. Patron privacy is a very strict rule of the library."

"Now listen to me, you old . . ."

"Martin." Miss Evalina placed her hand on his shoulder. She got up and took Mrs. Chancy's hand. "Louise, we've been friends for a long time, and you know how I feel about breaking rules. But this could be important. Very important."

Mrs. Chancy stood rigid for just a minute; then her shoulders slumped. "But, Eva, I could lose my job."

"I know, I know. And maybe even for nothing. But if there is the slightest chance of any leads being on that computer . . . well, Louise dear, what's more important? Your job or Aggie's life?"

Miss Jane gasped, and the rest of us drew in our breaths sharply. This was the first time anyone had actually voiced the fear we all shared.

Mrs. Chancy stared in shocked silence then bit her lip.

"But all I know about computers is how to turn them on and off. I have an instruction sheet for anyone who wants to get online, but that's it."

"What'd I tell you? It didn't do a blame bit of good to come down here." Martin gave a disgusted grunt.

"Have no fear, my friends. At school they used to call me 'Hack' for short." Benjamin stepped over to Mrs. Chancy. "Just point me in the right direction."

Now why didn't that surprise me? It was probably the reason he got kicked out of the first two colleges he attended. Although to be fair, he did graduate with honors from the third.

As we drove back to the lodge, I didn't know whether to be relieved or disappointed, and from the expressions on all the other faces, I suspected they felt the same way.

A stress-filled sigh gushed out of Miss Evalina. "So, where do we go from here?"

Miss Georgina sniffled, and Miss Jane sighed a twin to Miss Evalina's.

As the tires slushed through the melting snow, I glanced at Benjamin out of the corner of my eye. Was that a smirk? I turned my head a little and took a closer look, ready to lambaste him, then winced. The grimace on his face was worry. Intense worry. A wash of burning tears made their way out of my eyes and down my cheeks. I'd held onto a tiny seed of hope that perhaps Miss Aggie was just having a golden age romance with someone she'd met online. But after finding nothing in her files but innocent shopping and bed-and-breakfast Web sites, that idea flew out the window. Of course she could have been doing research for herself and someone she'd met right here in Cedar Chapel or some place near. My mind flashed back to the magazine on her nightstand. Could she possibly have gone away? With someone or even alone? But surely she would have taken at least a change of clothing, and according to the ladies, nothing was missing except what she was wearing and the diamonds. An involuntary shiver ran through my body. It seemed likely Miss Aggie was in the hands of the bank robbers, just as Sheriff Turner suspected.

The next couple of days seemed to crawl by, and I don't think I'd ever seen a more dejected group of people. On Saturday Martin spent a couple of hours at the bowling alley, and Frank hung out at the candy store some, but he'd even given up playing around with his beloved ham radio. For the most part, we all stayed at the lodge. None of the lady boarders would so much as step outside alone. We all went to our respective church services on Sunday morning then moped around all afternoon.

We scoured Ben's paper for news, although if any occurred, I hoped he'd let us know first. Calls to the sheriff's office didn't get us anything but irritated promises that they'd let us know if they found out anything. Like I believed that. When Martin ended up with ringing ears from the phone being slammed down, I finally suggested that we should perhaps limit our calls . . . to maybe three or four a day.

On Monday morning I was in the basement sorting through laundry when the phone rang.

"Victoria, it's for you!" Miss Jane could be heard on the moon when she wanted.

I trudged up the basement stairs, telling myself

for the umpteenth time that I really needed to install an extension in the basement.

Miss Jane stood in the kitchen, her eyes bright. She held out the phone to me and whispered, "It's the sheriff."

"Hello, Sheriff Turner."

"Victoria, I need you and everyone at the lodge to get down to the station. There's an FBI agent here who wants to talk to you. He wants your statements."

"Right now? I'm in the middle of doing laundry."

"Yes, right now. You've been driving me crazy wanting to be in the middle of everything, and now you want to finish your laundry?" I could almost see his round face getting red. Of course he was right.

"Sorry, Sheriff. I'll get everyone together and we'll be there as quickly as possible. Do you need Corky, too? Or just the ones who live here?"

A sigh of exasperation came through the earpiece. "Everyone means everyone, Victoria."

"Okay, okay. Corky, too. Bye."

"What does he want me for?" Corky looked nervous, which made me wonder, but he helped me round everyone up. I really needed an intercom.

Frank was at the candy shop, so we stopped there on the way to pick him up.

The FBI agent turned out to be a very nice gentleman who immediately put me at ease. He took our statements individually and methodically and sent us on our way, leaving me a little bit let down.

We stopped outside the courthouse and just looked at each other.

Miss Jane stomped her small shoe on the sidewalk. "Were you all expecting more than that? You'd think they could have at least let us know how the investigation's going."

"Ha! That's because there is no investigation to speak of," Martin said. "All those honchos do is use up our tax money and get nothing done."

"Do you really think so, Martin? They aren't doing anything about it?" Miss Georgina's voice quivered.

Martin gave a little embarrassed grin and didn't answer.

I placed my arm around Miss Georgina's plump shoulders and gave her a comforting little pat.

"Of course they're doing something. It just takes time to get everything organized. They'll find Miss Aggie and the bank robbers, too."

"I say we do something ourselves," Frank retorted. "I'm tired of holing up at home waiting for some word. Aggie'd expect us to find her."

"You're absolutely right, Frank. I've been thinking the same thing." Was Miss Evalina agreeing with Frank?

I felt five pairs of eyes focused on me. Okay, how I handled this would be a turning point in more ways than one, I suspected. An unfamiliar spurt of confidence welled up in me, and once more I felt like a sleuth in one of my mystery books. Maybe Dame Agatha's Tuppence Beresford.

"I agree. Let's go over to the bank and talk to Phoebe Sullivan."

I didn't feel much like Tuppence, though, as we walked two by two down the street then filed in through the bank door one by one.

I spotted Phoebe right away. Blond curls bobbed as she nodded to Mrs. Tyson and counted out the lady's money.

A fresh-out-of-business-school teller, Phoebe had faced the barrel end of the robber's gun. Her gumption inspired me, and I looked on in admiration as she conducted her business as though nothing at all had happened to her.

We stood to the side and waited until Mrs. Tyson turned away, and then we walked over.

Phoebe look up, startled, as we crowded up to her window.

"Good morning, Victoria, Miss Jane." I wondered if she would recite every name, but she stopped and smiled, her eyes scanning us all, resting a little longer, perhaps, on Corky. Interesting. Of course, Corky wasn't bad looking if you liked the type. Tight, reddish brown curls covered his head, and his stocky, muscular frame seemed to exude masculinity as he stood there grinning.

"May I help you?" The girl was blushing, for heaven's sake.

“Phoebe,” I spoke quietly, “do you have a minute to talk to us about the robbery?”

Her eyes widened, and she appeared ready to bolt. Then she took a deep breath and squared her shoulders. “I’m not supposed to talk about it to anyone except the sheriff and FBI agent.”

“Well . . . ,” I began.

Corky sidled up to the window and flashed what he probably thought was an irresistible smile. Apparently he was right, because before I knew what had happened, we were drinking coffee at the Mocha Java coffee shop down the street. Corky had pulled three tables together, so we were quite cozy.

Phoebe sat directly across from me. “It was time for my break anyway,” she said.

“Phoebe, as you probably know, it seems likely Miss Aggie was kidnapped by the robbers. If there’s anything at all you can tell us, no matter how seemingly insignificant, it might help us find her.”

“All right, Victoria. I’ll tell you what I remember.” She bit her lip and glanced sideways at Corky, who leaned on the table with one elbow. He smiled encouragingly.

“I’ve already told all this to the sheriff and that FBI agent. Mr. Hurley was speaking to me about some deposits when three men came bursting through the front door. They were wearing ski masks, and before I had time to think, one of them shoved Mr. Hurley out of the way and started yelling at me to give him all the money in the drawer. He was waving a gun in my face, and I was so scared I just froze." Phoebe stopped, picked up a glass of water with trembling hands, and took a long drink.

"He kept shaking the gun in my face and threatening to shoot if I didn't do what he said. And there was another masked guy guarding the door. He had a gun, too. I was so scared. I shoved money in the bag as fast as I could. He yanked it out of my hand and ran out, followed by the other two. I was the only teller at work that morning, so my drawer was pretty full. I found out later that another robber forced Mr. Hurley back to the vault and made him open the safe. The bank officers won't tell us how much was stolen, but I know it was a lot."

The pitch of Phoebe's voice had gotten higher, and she picked nervously at a napkin. Corky glared at me and looked as if he wanted to stop my line of questioning.

"It's okay, Phoebe." I patted her hand. "Take a deep breath."

She closed her eyes and breathed deeply.

"There. Better?"

She nodded.

"I know you were really frightened, and the men wore masks. But did you notice anything about them that seemed familiar?"

The girl bit her lip and shook her head. "I'm sorry. I was so scared. It's a good thing we have security cameras, because I couldn't even tell the sheriff how tall they were or anything. And the one at my window was yelling so loudly, I don't think I could identify his voice."

Martin expelled a sound of exasperation. "Come on, girl. Surely there's something you can tell us."

"Leave her alone, Martin. If she didn't recognize him, she didn't recognize him." At Corky's insistent tone, Martin flopped back with a surly look on his face.

We thanked Phoebe and walked her back to the bank, where we came face-to-face with Sheriff Turner and the agent.

"What do you think you're doing here?" The sheriff's voice boomed with anger. Then he spotted Phoebe. "Are you badgering a witness?"

"Oh, don't get so riled up, Bob," Miss Evalina said. "We're not hurting anything. We're just concerned about Aggie."

He yanked his hat off. "Well, Miss Swayne, I'm sorry. I know you're worried about your friend. But I just can't have a bunch of amateurs botching up the investigation." He clenched his hat between his hands. I would have been willing to bet about anything right then that Sheriff Turner was one of Miss Evalina's ex-students. When he realized what he was doing, he scowled and crammed his hat back on his head. "Besides that, someone could get hurt. Now, I want the whole lot of you to stay out of law enforcement business before I throw you all in jail for obstructing justice." With that, he shoved through the door.

The FBI agent gave us a curt nod and followed the sheriff into the bank.

After lunch, which Corky magically supplied at our usual time, I went to the laundry room and finished sorting. I put a load in the washer then ambled up to the front parlor and started dusting around the window seals. The doorbell rang, and I opened the door to find Benjamin standing there.

Most of the seniors were taking naps, but Frank and I sat in the small parlor and told Benjamin the morning's events.

Benjamin shook his head. "The poor kid. I tried to get her to talk to me the day after the robbery, but she wouldn't even look at me. Just gave me a nervous little smile and walked off."

"It must have been terrible for her." I couldn't hold back a sigh. "I do wish she could have remembered more, though."

Frank reached over and patted my hand. "Don't worry. Aggie's gonna turn up fine and dandy."

"Thanks, Frank. I wish I could be sure."

A trilling sound startled me, and I realized it was coming from Ben's pocket. He gave me an apologetic smile as he pulled his cell phone out. *That's something else I probably need. Why haven't I bought a cell phone yet?*

"Ben Grant here." He paused. "Is that right?

Thanks, Steve. I'll get right on it." He pocketed the phone and was halfway to the door before he remembered to call back over his shoulder. "Another bank's been robbed. Gotta go."

"Where, Benjamin? Could I go—?" But the door closed on my words.

Frank decided to go do some personal shopping, and I headed for the basement, waving at Corky as I passed through the kitchen. As I threw the load into the dryer, my mind suddenly grabbed onto a thought that had been in the back of my mind for the last couple of days. What did I really know about Corky? Only a couple of months earlier, he'd answered my ad after Grandma's longtime cook retired. He'd had good references, but that didn't really prove anything. His meals were culinary delights, without fail, but what about his character? I went back up to the kitchen and paused, watching him from the doorway as he wiped the counter.

He started as he turned and saw me. "Dinner's ready to go into the oven. There's salad and dessert in the fridge." When I didn't answer, he wrinkled his brow. "Is anything wrong?"

"Oh. No. No, of course not. I was just daydreaming. Thank you, Corky."

He grinned and waved as I headed upstairs.

When I got to my room, I flopped down in my easy chair, random thoughts whirling in my head. Miss Aggie couldn't have disappeared into thin air. Surely clues waited to be found somewhere.

I took a notebook and pen out of my side table. Okay, what did I have so far? Were there any real suspects? Who had motive? I started to write.

Suspects and Motives

1. The bank robbers: Maybe. If Miss Aggie saw their faces when they left the bank. Could she have recognized them?
2. Frank Cordell: Could be. If he was still bitter after all these years over the broken romance.
3. Corky: He seems innocent enough, but why was he listening at the door the day she was kidnapped? What motive could he possibly have? (To be looked into.)
4. Unknown Internet acquaintance: Could Benjamin have missed something? Have my suspicions been right all along?

A tingling began on the top of my head, continuing down my body until it became a full-fledged shudder. I flung the notebook away from me and jumped up. I rushed down the hall, unlocked Miss Aggie's door, and went in. Closing the door softly, I walked over to her dresser, touching the items on top. They were neat and clean. The ivory-handled hairbrush rested next to a hand mirror, obviously a matched set and very old. Some of the bristles were gone from the brush. I wondered why she hadn't replaced it. I had come upstairs once to speak to

Miss Aggie about something, and she had sat at this very dresser, brushing her long veil of hair, still jet black at her age. . . . I carried the brush over to the small wicker rocking chair and sat down. Tears trickled down my face. *Oh, Miss Aggie. Where are you? Are you suffering somewhere?* A sob rose from deep down inside me.

I heard a soft sound from the hall outside, and the door opened.

"Now, child, don't take on so." Miss Evalina walked to my side and knelt down on the floor, her knees giving off a little crackling sound. She reached up and smoothed my hair, and I took her hand in mine.

"You were right. Grandma would have done more. I'm so sorry I can't find Miss Aggie."

"Honey, you're doing everything you can. And I shouldn't have made that remark about Caroline. I can't imagine what she could have done that you haven't already." Gently she pulled her hand from mine and straightened herself up with the help of the chair arm.

"Let's go get some tea. We'll think more clearly with a cup of hot tea in our hands."

I stood up, replaced the hairbrush, and followed her from the room.

I hate it when I cry. For one thing, I end up with a splitting headache which only time in bed, hot packs, and sinus medicine can cure. But the main reason I hate it is because I always wake up the next day looking like W. C. Fields, the old actor with the red nose. Martin has all his old movies, and when he gets in a W. C. mood, he insists on watching them in the recreation room so we can all "enjoy" them. Of course, he's not fooling anyone. It's really the big-screen TV he's interested in.

The morning after my emotional breakdown in Miss Aggie's room, Corky took one look at me, poured a cup of hot, black coffee, and led me to the kitchen table. I was so grateful, I decided maybe I should take him off my suspect list. After my second cup of the hot brew, the throbbing pain had subsided somewhat. While Corky prepared breakfast, I headed to my office to print out some recipes for the baking he and I had promised to do for the Christian Women's Foundation's annual bake sale. Just as I pushed the POWER button on my computer, the phone rang.

"Good morning, Cedar Lodge. May I help you?" I hoped I sounded cheerier than I felt.

"Hi, Victoria. It's me." Well, wonder of wonders. Benjamin had called me by my full name for a change.

"Hi, Benjamin. You didn't tell us where the new robbery was." I was still miffed about that.

"Oh. Sorry. I was in a hurry. It was in Middle Point."

"Wow. That's close." I frowned. How many more would they hit before they were caught? "Do they have any leads? Was it the same robbers?"

"Probably. It was pretty much the same. Three men wearing ski masks. One held up the teller, one stood guard, and the other one hit the safe. Only this time a deputy was in the employee lounge. He came out and took a pot shot as they left the bank. Clipped one of them. They're not sure how bad, but the owner of the shoe shop down the street told me one of them was holding his hand and yelling his head off."

"Hmmm. Well, I hope they catch them soon. If they have Miss Aggie, they'd better not have hurt her." My words presented a mental picture I could hardly stand. "Oh, Benjamin, isn't there anything we can do? I feel so helpless."

"That's why I called. I'm heading back over there to sniff around some more. Wanna come along?"

I hesitated. Corky and I really needed to get started with the baking soon. And why would Benjamin invite me along anyway? But who cared why? And the baking could wait until afternoon. I wasn't about to pass up this chance.

"Sure. I just need to grab my coat. I'll wait for you on the porch."

He got there just as I stepped out the door. As I walked to the car, he got out, went around to the passenger's side, and opened the door for me with a flourish.

"Why, thank you, Benjamin. I didn't know you had a gentlemanly streak in you."

He flashed me that irritating, sarcastic little side grin of his. "Hate to disappoint you, Vickie. This door is hard to close from the inside."

I seethed inwardly, feeling my face burn. Okay, another point for him. This was getting tiresome.

The drive to the quaint tourist town of Middle Point took only ten minutes. The storefronts on the downtown square gave an old-world ambience to the area, although the town itself wasn't as old as Cedar Chapel.

Benjamin parked on a side street, and we walked around the corner and down to the bank. As we stepped through the door, several employees glanced up nervously before returning to their work. Apparently we didn't look like bank robbers. However, a security guard ambled our way and stopped just close enough to make sure we saw him.

Ben headed for a teller window and flashed a charming smile at the elderly woman behind it. She returned it with a beaming one of her own. "May I help you?"

"I certainly hope so," Benjamin said as he removed his wallet from his pocket. He showed her his newspaper credentials. "I'm Benjamin Grant from over in Cedar Chapel. I'd like to get some information on the robbery."

"Oh. Well, I wasn't here when it happened." She gave a vague wave toward the offices on the other side of the room. "If you'll take a seat over there, I'll see if I can get someone to help you."

Thereby dismissed, we did as directed. A few minutes later, a gray-haired lady wearing a tailored business suit appeared. She stood in front of our chairs and stared us down for a moment before speaking.

"I'm afraid no one can speak to you right now. Our bank president is busy and has instructed us not to discuss the matter with anyone. You'll have to get your information from the police department." She waited for Benjamin's response, obviously braced for an argument, and looked a little surprised when he simply stood up and thanked her.

We left the bank, and I threw a questioning glance his way. It wasn't like Benjamin to give up so easily.

"I'd hoped the girl that worked yesterday would be here," he said. "When I realized there was a different teller, I didn't really expect to get anything from them."

The smell of coffee and bacon assailed me as we passed a small café, and I regretted not taking the time for breakfast.

“So,” I asked, “do you want to talk to the police?”
“Nah. I talked to them yesterday and interviewed a few people on the street. I’ll just have to use what I have for now and follow up tomorrow.”
We turned onto the side street, and when we reached the car, I stopped and stared at a pickup parked a few doors down. My mouth dropped open, and I tugged at Benjamin’s sleeve.
“That’s Frank Cordell’s truck. What’s he doing at a pawn shop?”
He glanced that way and shrugged. “Who knows? Checking out tools or rifles, maybe.”
“Hmmm.” I could feel my eyes starting to squint, but I didn’t care. “I’m not so sure about that. What if he’s trying to sell Miss Aggie’s diamonds?”
He gave me a look of incredulity and snorted as he opened the car door for me.
“Don’t be ridiculous. Frank’s loaded. Well, maybe not loaded. But he’s not hurting any.”
I tossed him an indignant glance as I got in and fastened my seat belt. I waited for him to slide in behind the steering wheel.
“I think you’re missing the point, Benjamin. I’m not concerned about the diamonds. What if he’s done something with Miss Aggie and now he’s trying to get rid of the evidence?”
He inserted the key in the ignition then turned to look at me. “I’m not sure I’m following you. If he did something with Aggie, why not just leave the diamonds on her instead of taking a chance?

And why in the world would he want to harm Aggie, anyway?"

"Well, how should I know?" I stormed. I hated it when he turned logical on me. "Maybe he's been holding a grudge all these years because of the rejection or something."

Benjamin shook his head and started the car. "Okay, we'll talk to him. Will that make you happy?"

I wasn't sure about happy, but at least it was something. I liked Frank, but if he'd harmed Miss Aggie, he wasn't getting away with it. And he'd find that out real soon.

A few minutes later we drove into Cedar Chapel. My stomach rumbled another reminder that I'd skipped breakfast.

Benjamin chuckled, turned onto the square, and pulled up in front of Perkins' Café. "I'm hungry, too. Is this okay?"

Hannah Perkins made the best pancakes and biscuits in town, so I wasn't about to complain. Even at midmorning the place was almost full. After stopping to say hello to several acquaintances, we found an empty booth near the back.

"Well, hello you two." I didn't like the speculative look Hannah darted at us as she placed menus on the table. "What can I get you? Just drinks or needing sustenance?"

"Coffee, please, Hannah," I said. "I don't need a menu. I'd just like a short stack, please."

Hannah gave me a wink and then turned to Benjamin. "How about you, Ben?"

"Same, I guess. Except make mine a full stack. Oh, and some sausage on the side." He grinned and handed her both menus.

After she walked away, Benjamin shot me a look of amusement. "This'll be all over town before two o'clock."

"What will?" I asked, making sure my voice was carefully nonchalant while knowing full well what he meant.

"Oh, you know." He waved his hand at me then pointed at himself. "You. Me. A cozy booth."

"Well, that's the silliest thing I ever heard of. We just stopped for breakfast. Why would anyone think anything about that?"

He laughed out loud. "Oh, I dunno. Maybe because your eyes are sparkling and you have this guilty look on your face."

I felt my mouth fly open. "Why, you . . . you . . ." Sensing a sudden quiet, I glanced up to see everyone in the café looking at me, most of them grinning.

I leaned forward and whispered, "If it wasn't for making a scene, I'd walk right out of here."

"Tsk, tsk. Think of the rumors that would start. Everyone would be talking about our lovers' spat." He reached over and patted my hand. "Don't worry, Vickie. It'll blow over in a day or two."

Before I could retort, Hannah waltzed up to our

table. She placed our coffee, a bowl of butter, and a large pitcher of syrup in front of us. She glanced from me to Benjamin, then back at me.

"This is just precious. I never would have thought you two would be together after all the fighting you did as kids. Just goes to show, you never can tell." She beamed at us and walked away. I heard a chuckle from behind me. Looking around, I spotted Junior Whitly two booths down, grinning.

"Hi, Victoria. Hi, Ben." He waved.

I sighed and mustered up a smile. I wouldn't get aggravated at Junior. I appreciated him too much. He'd been keeping the exterior of Cedar Lodge looking good in his spare time. Junior was, as they say, a jack-of-all-trades.

I turned back around and faced Benjamin. He sat with a very satisfied expression on his face. Sort of like the proverbial cat who ate the canary. I, of course, was the canary.

We waited in the great room because I decided sitting in the front parlor with Benjamin would be much too cozy. Especially since it seemed all the ladies had chosen this day to finally venture to the senior center. The first time since Miss Aggie's disappearance. I wanted to tell Benjamin I could handle Frank myself and then send him on his way, but the thought of confronting the old gentleman with my suspicions made my stomach churn. I shivered. If Frank didn't get back soon, I'd have to build a fire.

Benjamin had made several attempts to start a conversation, but my silence finally discouraged him. He sauntered around the room, examining the portraits on the wall and whistling to himself. I wished he'd stop the infernal whistling. He stopped in front of the fireplace, gazing up at the portrait above the mantel. "Is this your great-great-grandfather?"

Okay. True, I didn't want to talk to Benjamin, but there were very few topics I'd rather discuss than my ancestors.

"Third great. That's Franklin Storm."

"Ah, the jailbird."

"Excuse me? Just what's that supposed to mean?"

He turned and gave me an "oh-so-innocent" glance.

"You know. Isn't he the one who got his freedom from prison by agreeing to work his way to America on a ship coming over from England? Indentured, too, I believe." He quirked one eyebrow and started to turn back to the picture.

I jumped up, fury rising in me. How dare he?

"For your information . . ." I stopped. "Well, okay, that's sort of how it was, but you don't have to be so insulting." I glared at him. "And for your information, debtors' prison wasn't all that uncommon, and he redeemed himself quite nicely."

For once, Benjamin looked contrite. "I'm sorry. I was just teasing. I know what a great man Franklin Storm was. He made many contributions to this area and the state, too, for that matter."

I exhaled and relaxed. "He built this room, you know. It was both the living and sleeping area. There was a covered walkway between it and the kitchen in back. Hunters came from miles around. Then my second great-grandfather, Josiah Storm, tore down the old kitchen and built the remainder of the first floor. Eventually, he added the second and third stories. When my great-grandfather, Henry Storm, inherited the estate, he shut down the hunting lodge and started selling off the land."

"Yes, I know." Benjamin was gazing at me rather fondly. I wanted to kick myself. Of course he knew. Everyone around here knew the story of my ancestors. Besides, now that I thought of it, I very clearly remembered bragging about my family to Benjamin when we were kids. And here I was, rambling on, making an utter fool of myself.

"I'm sorry," I mumbled. "Of course you know."

"It's okay. I never get tired of hearing about the history of Cedar Chapel and especially this house. It must have been exciting in its heyday. But Henry Storm had an eye for the future. He wanted a town. Cedar Chapel would more than likely have become another ghost town if not for your great-grandfather's desire for community."

Yeah, and if it hadn't been for the stock market

crash, I'd be a millionaire. I sighed as I did every time the thought crossed my mind, and then I turned my attention back to Benjamin.

"We only go back two generations, to my grandfather," he said. "My ancestors weren't from around here."

"I know. I remember the story you told me about your grandpa. He was a circuit preacher, right?"

"Right. Preached on the weekends. Worked for Mr. Patterson at the newspaper through the week."

"Then married the boss's daughter?"

"You do remember." He smiled and glanced at his watch. "I'm afraid I'm going to have to—"

The front door opened, and Frank and Martin walked into the foyer. They saw us standing in the great room and joined us.

Hmmm. If Frank had something to do with Miss Aggie's disappearance, I wondered if Martin was in on it, too? "Hi, Frank. Martin. Didn't know you two were together," I said.

"We weren't. Frank just stopped by the center and brought me home." Martin glanced at us then at the cold hearth. "What are you two standing in here in the cold for?"

I blushed and avoided the question. "The ladies didn't come with you?"

"Nah," Frank growled. "Jane drove that broken-down piece of junk she calls a car."

"Oh well, it's not all that bad." I said it but

didn't really believe it. Miss Jane's ancient Cadillac should have been junked years ago, but she refused to part with it.

"Don't know why Eva would rather ride in that junk heap than with me," he muttered.

Ignoring him, I darted a quick glance at Benjamin, who nodded at me and turned to Frank.

"Frank, could Victoria and I talk to you for a minute?"

"Sure." He waved at Martin, who left the room.

"What's up?" Frank asked. "You find out something about Aggie? Is that it?"

Benjamin and I looked at each other. He cleared his throat. "No, nothing like that. We saw your truck outside the pawn shop in Middle Point and wondered what you were . . . doing."

Benjamin looked uncomfortable, and to be honest, once I heard the words spoken, I was a little bit embarrassed as well.

"Huh?" Frank looked confused. "What in tarnation business is it of yours what I was doing at the pawn shop?" He gave us a fierce glare and slammed out of the room. I wasn't sure if he was angry or guilty.

"That went well," Benjamin said with a sheepish smile on his face.

"Yeah, but if he's innocent, why'd he get so mad?"

"Well, let's see now. You think maybe he was mad because we were prying into his business? I know I would have been."

"You don't have to be so sarcastic, Benjamin. But I guess you're right."

Benjamin chuckled. "Did I really hear you say I was right? See you later, Vickie."

I headed upstairs as he walked out the front door. As I reached Miss Aggie's room, I stopped. Would it really hurt just to take a peek at the diary and letters? What if there was a clue of some kind there that could explain Miss Aggie's disappearance? With guilt stabbing at my heart, I opened the door and stepped inside. I stepped over to the little bedside table and laid my fingers softly on the diary, my heart pounding. Resolutely, I picked up the book then retrieved the packet of letters from the closet.

Returning to my room, I sat in the recliner, placed the letters in the drawer of the side table, and opened Miss Aggie's diary.

May 15, 1942

My fifteenth birthday. I can't believe it. I got so many gifts from Mums and Father and all the others, I'll be writing thank-you notes for a month. What a bother. Still, Mums says a lady always acknowledges each and every gift. And I do so want to be a lady. I think, of all my gifts, this little journal may be my favorite. Finally, a place where I can bare my soul without fear of intrusion. Such as my feelings when Tyrone Adams kissed my hand today. I know he was just being kind, but oh, he is so handsome, I can't help but dream of the possibility of his caring for me someday. Although I suppose he is a little too old for me. He must be at least twenty.

I smiled. It was difficult to imagine such a young Miss Aggie. The first half of the diary was much the same. She hadn't really kept up with it regularly, with months going by without a word, then paragraphs full of girlish gushing about one boyfriend or another. I yawned and had about decided to put the diary aside when a familiar name caught my attention. From the date on the page, Miss Aggie would have been eighteen.

January 16, 1946

Frank Cordell came home today. How different he seems. I always thought him a little dull before he went off to Europe to fight the Nazis, whoever they are. Apparently, his experiences in the war have changed him greatly. I do so envy anyone who can get away from this boring place.

Eva threw a coming-home party for him last night, and of course I was invited. The moment I laid eyes on Frank, my heart nearly stopped beating. I know he feels the same way. I could see it in his eyes. But of course, he wouldn't say anything, since he and Eva have practically been engaged since they were ten. At least in her eyes. And I always thought in his, too. Of course, he did give her that ring before he went to war. But who knows? Boring little Eva may be in for a big surprise.

Eva? Was she talking about Miss Evalina? The ladies mostly called her Eva. But of course, that wasn't an uncommon name back then.

I continued to read, and my heart almost broke for the young Evalina, who lost her only love at the hands of a spoiled little rich girl. A very short-lived romance. But one that evidently had a lasting effect on the players in the story.

February 2, 1946

Oh, I never would have imagined Father would speak to me so. When he saw Frank's ring, he actually tried to rip it off my finger. I finally took it off, but I've hidden it in my wardrobe. Father will be sorry. Frank and I will run away together. Only Father is right about one thing. Frank is awfully poor. What if he can't afford to take care of me?

July 20, 1946

Frank has been in Kansas City for months. Yesterday his mother told me he was working in a candy factory. I wish he would write to me more often. Father has ruined my life and I'll never forgive him.

Then an entry dated a year later:

So much for the great love of my life. Frank has married the daughter of his employer. Oh well. I lost interest in him months ago. Johnny Shepherd is much more fascinating and is quite rich. But Frank better not ask me for his ring back, because he's not getting it.

I closed the diary and sat, pondering. Aggie, Frank, Evalina. There was more to this story, I was sure.

And if it had anything to do with Miss Aggie's disappearance, I wouldn't give up until I got to the bottom of it.

Call me nosy, but I could hardly wait for the opportunity to talk to Miss Evalina. Besides, I really needed to make sure she wasn't holding a grudge against Miss Aggie. I restrained myself all afternoon and evening, however, because by the time I finished helping Corky with the baking, boxing, and wrapping of dozens of cookies, pies, and cakes, Miss Evalina had escaped to bed, complaining of a headache.

The next morning, I found the perfect opportunity after breakfast. I was in my office, going over accounts, when Miss Georgina and Miss Jane appeared in the doorway.

"Victoria, we're going for a drive. Can we do anything for you while we're out?" Was that a bit of excitement in Miss Jane's voice? Maybe a little too much for a morning drive. I looked from one lady to the other. Umm-hmm. Miss Georgina's face was several shades redder than usual, and it wasn't duc to hcr makcup this time.

I laid my pcn on the desk and turned off my computer screen.

"All right, you two. You're up to something." I raised my eyebrows in mock accusation, and both ladies tittered.

Miss Georgina gave a nervous little frown. "Should we tell her, Jane?"

Miss Jane sighed loudly. "Well, all right, but she's just going to try to talk us out of it. Don't try to talk us out of it, Victoria, because we're going."

I hated it when they talked about me like I wasn't sitting right there. "Oo–kay. Going where?"

"Well, I just can't stand sitting here doing nothing any longer. It's time someone searched the back roads around town for Aggie. You know, in case she had a wreck or got thrown from a car or some-thing." At this, fear washed over Miss Jane's face. But she immediately composed herself, pressed her lips together, and tapped her toe on the hardwood floor.

"I'm sure the sheriff has already searched," I said.

"Maybe he has and maybe he hasn't. But I'm not taking any chances."

"All right, then. I don't see any harm in looking. You ladies be careful, though, and please don't drive too far out of town."

"We're not children, Victoria," Miss Georgina said. "We've taken care of ourselves for some time now." Her glare was indignant, but I knew it was more a cover for her fear than anything else.

"I'm sorry, Miss Georgina. I know you're both quite capable of taking care of yourselves."

She sniffed but was apparently mollified, because she gave me a hug before they exited the room.

I sat for a moment, wondering if I should go with them. It wouldn't be at all good if Miss Georgina got into one of her fear-induced tizzies while they were out and about. She'd seemed okay, though. I was a little bit surprised they hadn't persuaded Miss Evalina to go along. But since they hadn't, maybe I should try to have that talk with her. I pushed my chair back and went to find her. She was nowhere downstairs, so I headed up to her room.

She invited me in, and as always, her antique-furnished room was warm and inviting. She graciously waved me to an overstuffed pale blue brocade sofa while she resumed her seat on a matching wingback chair.

She looked at me with a sad smile. "I've been expecting you. You've read the diary, haven't you?"

"Yes."

"So what did Aggie say about me? About Frank?"

"She wrote about Frank's coming-home party. About their growing attraction for each other. Some of the same things you told us before." I waited, wondering if she knew how much was revealed in that diary.

An expression of nostalgia washed over her face. "It was here, you know."

"What was here?"

"The party. Our home wasn't nearly large enough for a party of that size. And I was almost frantic because I knew everyone would expect an invitation to Frank's coming-home party."

She brushed a tear from her cheek. "Caroline was a new bride at the time. A very young bride. Your grandfather had brought her home to the lodge, and she loved it here. We'd become best friends, very quickly. She talked to your great-grandmother and they suggested the party be held here. Mrs. Storm insisted I be hostess that evening, even though they wouldn't let me pay one penny for anything. You come from a long line of kind and gracious people, Victoria. I'm happy to see you following their example."

I bit my lip. I couldn't allow her sweet words to keep me from what I needed to do.

"According to the entries in the diary, Miss Aggie very coldheartedly set out to win Frank away from you." She flinched, but I continued. "She had some pretty nasty things to say about you, Miss Evalina. Would you please tell me from your viewpoint what happened?"

She lifted her chin slightly and looked me in the eye. "No, dear. I won't."

Surprise made me speechless for a few seconds.

"But Miss Evalina, there are things in that diary that could indicate a motive for you to . . ." I stopped.

"To what? To kill Aggie? To spirit her away somewhere? Really, Victoria. If I'd wanted revenge, I'd have pursued it years ago." The disdain in her voice wasn't directed at me so much as at the circumstances, but I felt myself blush.

"Please, Miss Evalina. Tell me your side of the story."

She drew herself up and stood. Walking to the door, she opened it, turned, and motioned. She was kicking me out?

"But, Miss Evalina . . ."

"That's all, Victoria. Believe whatever you choose. I'm not discussing this."

I walked out the door, and she shut it firmly behind me.

Well, I handled that nicely. I stood in the hallway for a moment, undecided about what my next move should be. A walk, perhaps. Maybe the brisk air would help me think.

Running upstairs, I yanked my coat from the closet and pulled a blue and white knit cap over my head.

The air outside was a little more than brisk. I shivered as the icy wind seemed to cut right through my puffy coat. I needed to get something heavier for Missouri winters. Wool or down. Miss Jane's car pulled into the drive before I had a chance to leave the porch, so I decided it was a sign from God for me to stay home.

Miss Georgina and Miss Jane piled out of the car, huffing and puffing like the little pigs' wolf. Miss Georgina opened the back door of the car. My mouth flew open, and I stood gaping at the humongous ball of hair, mud, and snow that limped across the walk.

When he saw me, he galloped up the porch steps. The next thing I knew, Monster Dog's paws were on my chest, and it was all I could do to keep my balance.

"Ooof!" I shoved and hit with both hands while a sandpaper tongue made circles and swipes all over my face.

Miss Jane came scurrying up the stairs. "Get down! Get down! Georgina, help me."

The creature flopped its forefeet down and started hobbling in circles around the three of us. Finally, I managed to grab the piece of rope dangling free from his neck and give it a jerk. The animal yelped and cowered at my feet with its head on its paws.

"What in the . . . where did . . . Miss Jane!" I sputtered as I tried to catch my breath.

"Sorry. We didn't know he'd get loose. I had him tied to the door handle on the other side."

"But what's he doing here? Where did you get him?"

"Could we go inside first, dear? It's freezing out here." She started to open the door, and I jumped forward and grabbed the doorknob before she could.

"Wait. Don't let that dog inside."

Miss Georgina's lips quivered. "But he'll freeze out here. We can't just let him freeze to death."

Okay. Okay. Think, Victoria.

I sighed. "All right. You two go on in, and I'll

take the dog around back. Tell Corky to unlock the outside basement door."

I tightened my hold on the rope as the two ladies slipped through the door.

"Okay, buddy, let's go." I yanked on the rope, and the dog got up and started licking me again, its long, pink tongue lapping furiously all over my hands. Oh well. I was tired of these gloves anyway. Pulling, coaxing, and dragging, I managed to get the animal to the back where Corky stood holding the basement door open. He took the rope and got the dog down the basement stairs, where he did his little circle dance again.

"Hey there, fellow, I'll bet you're hungry, aren't you?" Corky rubbed the dog's big ugly snout between his hands and then looked at me. "You can go on up. I'll bring him something to eat and drink."

"Thanks. I'm going up all right. I think there's an explanation coming."

As I started up the stairs, the dog whined and tried to follow. Just what I needed. A hairy, slobbery creature who wanted to be my friend. Corky held him down until I made it through the kitchen door.

"But, Victoria, we couldn't leave him out there on a country road to starve. It was obvious someone dropped him off and left him to fend for himself."

We sat around the kitchen table drinking coffee. Martin had joined us. I had no idea where Frank was. Corky stuck his head through the door.

"We have a problem here. There's dried blood matted in the dog's coat, and there seems to be a tender spot on his left hind leg. I think he needs to see a vet."

Miss Jane and Miss Georgina murmured sympathetically. I just stared. What next?

"That explains the limp," I said. "Does he seem to be in much pain?"

"Only when I touch the leg. But it needs to be checked out. Actually, it looks to me like he's been grazed by a bullet."

Great. The closest vet was down in Branson and that was a good thirty miles of curving, icy back roads.

"Take him to Clyde Foster," Martin suggested.

"Clyde Foster? He's not a vet, is he?" Clyde owned the local pet shop, and a meaner old grouch I'd never seen.

"Nah, but he's done most of the doctoring on the animals in his shop for years," Martin said with a smirk. "Too cheap to pay a vet except in really bad cases."

"Are you sure, Martin?" To be honest, I didn't relish the idea of going into Mr. Foster's shop. He used to scare the daylights out of me when I was a child.

"It's true," said Miss Jane. "A lot of people take their pets to him when they don't want to drive to Branson."

I supposed there was no getting around it. I

asked Corky to put the dog in the van and tie him to anything he could find. When I arrived at the pet shop, I yanked on the rope and struggled to get him into the store.

The bell over the door clanged.

"Whatzit? Whatzit?" I jumped as something shrieked in my ear. Mr. Foster's parrot sat on a high perch right beside the door.

Mr. Foster came through the door at the back of the room. "Shut up, stupid bird," he yelled.

I felt the familiar dread as the sour-faced old man came forward. The bird jumped onto his outstretched arm, and he carried him to an enormous wheeled cage in the corner. When he opened the cage door, the bird waddled inside. So far, Mr. Foster hadn't acknowledged my presence. I cleared my throat, and he tossed me and the dog a look that shouted *Get outta here.*

"What do you want?" he snapped.

"Ummm." I stopped and licked my lips. "This dog is a stray and seems to have something wrong with his leg. Could you look at it?"

"Well, bring him back to the other room." He started walking to the door through which he'd come, and I followed, dragging Monster Dog behind me. I looked down at him. *You owe me, mister. Big time.* He returned my gaze with sad eyes, almost as though he could read my thoughts.

The examination revealed a wound that Mr. Foster stated might or might not have been caused by a bullet, and was at least a week old. Mr. Foster cleaned and bandaged it. He gave me some ointment to put on it for a few days to prevent infection and informed me, with a grunt, that was all he could do.

I thanked him, paid him the small amount he asked for, and started home, this time with the dog sitting on the seat beside me. After all, he'd been good, and who knew how he'd gotten that wound? Back at the lodge, I grabbed some old blankets and made him a comfortable bed in the basement, making sure the heat vents were open. Then I patted him on the head and went back upstairs.

"Your lunch is in the warming oven," Corky said over his shoulder as he placed dishes in the dishwasher.

"Where is everyone?" I asked.

"I think they all went up to their rooms after lunch. Except Martin. He's in the rec room watching his favorite."

Hmmm, so the rescuers apparently had decided their charge was in good hands with me and went up to take naps. Well, I liked that.

I ambled into the rec room to find Martin snoozing in a recliner while, on the screen, a black-and-white movie starring the great W. C. played. I went out and closed the door softly behind me.

I tiptoed up the stairs. Maybe a nap wasn't such a bad idea. Once in my room, though, I spotted my list of suspects lying on the bedside table. I sat in my chair and looked it over. Beside Frank Cordell's name, I added a question: *What was Frank Cordell doing at a pawn shop? Selling diamonds, perhaps?*

I sat and pondered for a few minutes then sighed and reluctantly added another name: *Evalina Swayne: Long-held jealousy and resentment? Why wouldn't she talk about her past relationships with Miss Aggie and Frank Cordell?*

Frowning, I shook my head. Was I making mountains out of molehills here? The more I thought about it, the more impossible it seemed and the more ridiculous I felt. Still . . .

No nearer a conclusion than before I started, I put the list in the drawer and took out the diary, open-ing it to the place where I'd stopped reading. I turned the page and sat up straight in surprise. The date on the next entry was more than twelve years later.

October 7, 1958

What a delightful surprise. If anyone besides me ever reads this, they will be terribly confused. Well, it'll serve them right for prying. Yesterday, while searching through the attic for old family photos, I came across this journal from my childhood. I don't know whether to laugh or cry for the silly young thing I was back then. I suppose many girls of that age and station in life are rather vain and selfish. I can forgive myself that. I should probably burn this because of the embarrassing entries, but I don't expect anyone to ever see them but me. It makes me feel rather nostalgic to write in this memento from my young and frivolous youth.

Actually, a lot of things are making me nostalgic today. I hope I'm doing the right thing, closing up the house. But I just want to live quietly and not be bothered with so-called friends and gentleman friends who turn out to want nothing but my money. The cottage will be a relief. Maybe I'll find peace there.

February 8, 1959

Forrest is furious that I refuse to sell the house. He has a buyer. But after investigating this buyer's business, I've found some rather shady dealings. I'm not going to be responsible for bringing riffraff into the area. The house can sit there and rot for all I care.

March 27, 1959

Forrest refuses to answer my letters or return my phone calls. He sent word he wanted to have nothing more to do with me. Forrest was the only family I had left. Now I'm truly alone.

There were a few other entries. Most of them ramblings. Then there were three entries from the following year.

April 14, 1960

I wonder if I'm losing my mind or so mething. I don't seem to want to leave the cottage anymore or see any of my old friends. Jane stopped by this morning, and I'm afraid I was rude to her. But I guess I have the right to be left alone if I'm so inclined.

May 3, 1960

Evalina says I'm acting like a sulking child and it's time I started living again. Perhaps she's right.

July 5, 1960

Yesterday I went to the Fourth of July Celebration in Cedar Chapel. I must admit it was nice seeing all my friends again. Evalina tells me a position is open for a history teacher at the high school and keeps insisting I apply for the job. She's been teaching English there for years and says it's a wonderful place to work. Maybe I'll do it.

That was the last entry. I closed the little diary. So Miss Evalina had helped Miss Aggie in spite of all she'd done. Was she really the friend she appeared to be, or could there be rage burning somewhere inside, even after all these years?

No one could ever accuse me of not liking animals, especially dogs. My precious chihuahua, Sparky, was a very important part of my life until he died a few years ago. But once Grandma turned the lodge into a boardinghouse, she had a strict no-animals-inside-the-house policy, and I didn't see any good reason to change it. It had worked for Grandma, so it was good enough for me. Everyone in the house knew it was a hard-and-fast rule. So, should I have expected to see a dog in my kitchen when I came down to breakfast? I think not. He spotted me the same moment I saw him, and before I could avoid him, those paws were on my chest and I was being treated, once more, to sloppy canine kisses.

"Ugh!" was all I could get out. I tried to wipe the slobber off my face, but he was determined to put more on.

"Buster, get down." Corky's command only served to excite the dog more.

"C'mon, boy." Corky grabbed him around the neck and pulled him off me as I gasped for air.

"What's he doing in the house?" I asked, wiping my face vigorously with the wet cloth Corky handed me.

"Sorry. I took him for a walk then put him back

in the basement, but he started howling. Guess he's not used to being alone."

"Well, he'll just have to howl until I can think what to do with him. I can't have him messing up the house."

The phone rang, and Corky picked it up. "Lodge," he said briefly, then, "Here, it's for you."

It was Benjamin calling to invite me to lunch.

"Lunch?"

"Yeah, you do eat lunch, don't you?" There was that sarcasm again.

"Well, of course I eat lunch. I just don't know why you want me to eat it with you."

"I thought maybe we could put our heads together and see what we have so far, but if eating with me is repugnant to you, that's okay."

I was a little bit embarrassed at my bad manners and a tinge disappointed that his invitation was a business one.

"Sorry, Benjamin. Lunch sounds great."

"Good. Pick you up around noon?"

"That's fine."

After breakfast, I spent the rest of the morning doing some work on the computer then went upstairs to freshen up and change. When I came back down, Benjamin stood waiting in the foyer.

After we got into the car and buckled up, Benjamin turned to me, eyes twinkling.

"Still have an aversion to Chinese food?"

"Not since I was twelve." I flashed him a bright

smile, secretly pleased he remembered that small detail about me from so long ago. "Chinese is fine, except we don't have a Chinese restaurant in town, you know."

"I thought, if you have a couple of hours, we could drive into Branson." He lifted one eyebrow. "Okay?"

"I guess so. But you have to promise to drive nice. The roads are still slippery. Better yet, why don't you pull over and let me drive?"

"Huh? I don't think so. I seem to remember you had to take your driver's test three times before you passed."

"Yeah, well, that was a long time ago. And I'm not going on these icy roads unless I'm in charge of the wheel. I just feel safer that way."

A definite scowl creased his brows, and he opened his mouth and then closed it.

Without saying a word, he tossed me the keys and got out of the car.

I laughed and scooted over behind the wheel. This wasn't the first time he'd given in to keep from having an argument, but it was rare. It felt good to win.

By the time we were two miles out of town, I regretted my rashness, but no way would I admit it. I tried to hide my nervousness as I drove the thirty miles of icy, winding roads to Branson.

As we drove past the Silver Dollar City entrance, Benjamin chuckled. "Remember the fun we used to have here with your grandparents?"

"Yeah. I also remember you sticking cotton candy in my hair."

"Really? I don't remember that."

"Sure you don't."

He chuckled. "Well, maybe I do, but I was just a kid, you know. A pretty bad one, I'll admit, but still, just a kid."

"Ah, so now you admit it wasn't an accident?" I could feel my mouth twisting.

"C'mon, Vickie. Are you going to hold grudges against me forever?"

As I drove on into town, I felt myself relaxing. Benjamin was right. Why couldn't I let those silly childhood pranks be bygones? After all, he did seem changed. And there was no denying he had a certain charm nowadays that I wasn't immune to.

He pointed out the restaurant, and I pulled into the parking lot.

A brightly clad hostess seated us and passed out menus. Candles flickered in the darkened room, lending an ambience of intrigue and romance to the setting. I glanced across the table. Benjamin's blue eyes appeared nearly black, and my imagination conjured up the dashing image of a pirate on the high seas.

He looked up and smiled as he caught me watching him. Blushing, I picked up my menu.

The food was delicious, and we ate mostly in silence, speaking occasionally about inconse-quen-tial things. Apparently, Benjamin didn't care to discuss serious matters while he enjoyed his food.

I watched in amusement as he attempted, unsuccessfully, to maneuver a bite of noodles to his mouth with chopsticks.

"You're holding them wrong, silly. Here, let me show you." I took my chopsticks and deftly picked up a small portion of rice, placing it in my mouth carefully. It had been a while since I'd used the instruments, and I didn't want to be on the receiving end of Benjamin's laughter.

I glanced at him with a triumphant smile to find him watching me with a strange expression. What was that look? Admiration? Longing? Surely not. Suddenly my pulse picked up speed, and I licked my lips. *Careful, Victoria. Don't fall for him.* It hadn't been that long since my breakup with Alan, whom I thought I'd love forever. That is, until I found out he was seeing someone else at the same time I wore his ring. Taking over Cedar Lodge had been like medicine for me, and over the past few months healing had taken place over both wounds. The breakup and losing Grandma. I didn't want to risk being hurt again.

I cleared my throat. "I've started a list of suspects. It's in my handbag if you'd like to see it."

"Sure," he said, moving his plate.

I retrieved the list and handed it over.

He nodded a few times and then looked up at me with an amused smile.

"What?" I demanded.

"Well, Victoria." He exhaled loudly and started again. "We've known Frank and Miss Evalina all our lives. How could you think either one of them would do something to Miss Aggie?"

I glared silently. It did sound ridiculous when put like that, but I wasn't about to admit it.

"I would think, Benjamin, in your profession, you would learn to be a bit more objective."

He laughed out loud, but when I shot him another glare, he scrunched his lips together. It was obvious he fought to keep a straight face. "I will admit, though," he said. "Corky could be a suspect."

"Oh, well, how kind of you to condescend to that at least."

"Ah, come on, Victoria. You know I'm kidding. I'm sorry I laughed, but it reminded me of the time you accused Pastor Thomas of stealing your dog."

"Well, how was I supposed to know you were the one who put Sparky on top of his shed? I should have known, though. After all, it hadn't been two weeks since you spray-painted him."

"Okay, I said I'm sorry. And I did clean Sparky up afterward. I know I was a scoundrel, though."

"Was? Now your meanness just comes out in other ways. Such as trying to make me feel stupid."

"What?" He looked surprised, and then his face softened. "Oh, sweetheart, I'd never in a million years think you were stupid. Don't you know how I feel about you?"

I sat frozen as his words pounded a cadence in my mind. *I can't do this again. I can't.*

I jumped up, grabbing my purse.

"I'm sorry, Benjamin. Can we leave now?" Without waiting for him to answer, I made a beeline across the floor. Shoving through the door, I headed for the parking lot. The car door was locked, of course, so I leaned against it and waited, breathing hard.

A few minutes later, Benjamin crossed the parking lot, slipping his wallet into his back pocket. He came around to the passenger side and unlocked my door then went around and unlocked his own.

"Ben, I'm sorry."

"Don't worry about it. It's my fault. I shouldn't have assumed you felt the same way I do."

We drove back to Cedar Chapel in silence. Miserable silence on my part. As we pulled into town, I stole a furtive look at Benjamin's face. His jaw was squared, and a muscle near his lip jumped. I'd not seen that look on his face since his mother left town without a word, when he and I were both fourteen.

He pulled up in front of the lodge and sat waiting for me to get out.

"Benjamin . . . ," I choked out.

He looked at me through pained eyes. "It's okay, Vickie. See you around."

Slowly, I slipped out of the car.

"See you, Benjamin," I whispered as he drove away.

I walked into the house, feeling like a heel for making Benjamin think I didn't care about him. Especially since it wasn't true. I actually cared a lot more for him than I was comfortable with. But I knew the pain that lay down that path.

I was starting across the foyer when out of the blue I was attacked. My feet slid out from under me on the waxed hardwood floor, and the next thing I knew I was on the floor, with Monster Dog grinning down at me.

I sat at the kitchen table and allowed Miss Georgina to doctor me, as she called it. She murmured sympathetically as she placed a cold compress on the bump I'd received when my head hit the floor. Miss Jane kept patting my shoulder, and Corky hovered over me as well, offering coffee, tea, and apologies.

"I thought he was asleep in the corner of the laundry room. I just slipped through the door with a basket of towels to fold when he shot past me. Before I could catch him, you came through the door."

"Okay, Corky, okay. I'm not really injured. It's just a little bump." I gently drew away from Miss Georgina's icy hands and laid the compress down on the table.

"But, sweetie, you really need to keep this on a little while longer to help the swelling go down."

“Thank you so much, Miss Georgina, but I’ll be fine now. In fact, I’m thinking about going to the fitness center for a soak in the hot tub. Anyone else want to go?”

Both ladies quickly took me up on the offer, and Miss Evalina decided to join us, too. When we drove into the parking lot at the fitness center, my stomach felt like a rock had taken up residence there. I’d just remembered Miss Aggie loved the hot tub.

“I think I’ll work out on the exercise machines before I get in the hot tub.” Miss Evalina’s expression dared anyone to object.

“Oh,” Miss Georgina piped up. “I think I will, too.”

Miss Jane nodded and away they went while I stood there with my mouth gaping. Shaking myself, I took off after them. I knew from experience I couldn’t stop them once they’d made up their minds about something, but maybe I could guide them a little bit. Keep them from getting hurt.

By the time I got to the weight-machine room, the three of them were already at the machines. Miss Evalina was adjusting the weights on the leg lift, and Miss Georgina and Miss Jane were seated at side-by-side rowing machines. I watched in amazement as the three of them went through their routines. I wondered how long this had been going on. For some time, by the looks of things.

After we came out of the hot tub, we went to the dressing room. As I was getting dressed, I heard a giggle and looked up to see three faces grinning smugly at me.

On the drive home, I finally couldn't hold it in any longer. "All right, you three. You've been keeping a secret. How long have you been working out on the machines? I mean, I think it's great, but . . ."

"We started last summer. I only wish Aggie had joined us." There was no humor in Miss Evalina's voice now.

Nor in Miss Jane's as she added, "No one is going to kidnap us without a fight."

I glanced at them, and tears welled up in my eyes. I loved these three almost as much as I'd loved Grandma. And the possibility of anything happening to them was unthinkable. I knew the amount of strength they could build up would never stop a strong man intent on harming them, but I was filled with admiration at their courage and determination.

Dinner that evening was rather quiet. Afterward, the boarders went to the recreation room. Corky cleaned up and started the dishwasher before he went home. I sat at the kitchen table and wrote letters to my parents.

I'd felt a little bit strange when Grandma's will revealed she'd left Cedar Lodge to me. My parents quickly assured me they'd known about it for years. She changed the will with their blessing. Everyone knew I loved Cedar Chapel and Grandma's boardinghouse. I'd spent all my holidays and summers here while I was growing up. My father had been occupied with his own business and interests. Mother had always hated Missouri and wouldn't think of living here. We'd seldom been able to even get her to visit.

When Miss Aggie disappeared, Dad had offered to come, but I knew he was in the middle of an important business venture at the time, so I convinced him I was fine. Mom was in Monte Carlo and called to gush over me. I wasn't surprised when she didn't offer to come. But tonight I found myself wishing they could know, for once, how much I needed them. I sealed the envelope and placed it on a small table with some others that needed to be mailed the next day.

I started to leave the room then on impulse opened the door to the basement and turned on the light. A whine met me as I walked down the stairs. The dog was curled up in a corner on his blanket bed. He got up and came to me cautiously, tail wagging. I knelt down and started rubbing his ears.

"How are you feeling, Buster Boy?" He wriggled and snuck his head farther up under my hand. For such a big animal, he could sure behave like a puppy. Even Sparky hadn't been this affectionate. I filled Buster's water bowl, gave him a final pat, and went upstairs, turning the light off behind me.

When my duties were all attended to and everyne was settled for the night, I went gratefully to my room, intent on relaxing with the book I'd started weeks ago and hadn't had a chance to read except in bits and pieces. However, a deluge of guilt feelings that I'd managed to hold at bay all afternoon and evening came pouring in with a vengeance.

I'd been terribly unfair to Benjamin. I should have explained. And I couldn't forget the look on his face. My mind went back to the lunch date. We really hadn't discussed the suspects at all after he'd conceded Corky might be one. As for that, it was hard for me to imagine Corky doing harm to anyone. He'd been so helpful lately. And the boarders all liked him. Well, that didn't necessarily mean anything. Most killers and kidnappers didn't go around broadcasting their evil deeds. I shivered. Miss Aggie might be kidnapped, but I refused to believe she was dead.

I took my shower and crawled under my down comforter. Picking up the book from my bedside table, I tried to concentrate on the words. Unfortunately, the book I'd chosen, by one of my favorite authors, was a chilling suspense novel. I got to the part where someone was being held in a basement filled with deadly spiders, and that was all I could handle. I closed the book with a bang and placed it back on the table. I'd finish it after Miss Aggie was found. And she would be found. Alive and well. With no nightmares about spiders to haunt her the rest of her life. *Please, God. Oh, Jesus. Miss Aggie's been gone a whole week. Please take care of her and let someone find her soon.*

When I came downstairs the next day, a curtain of gloom greeted me. Breakfast was silent and somber, and a veil of apathy hung over the room. After we cleared the dishes, the boarders moved to the parlor and sat there barely speaking to one another. Even the dog was in a crummy mood, rolling over and ignoring me when I went down to the basement to wash some towels.

By the time lunch was over, I'd reached my limit of sighs, moans, and general grumpiness. I remembered Miss Aggie's letters and decided this would be as good a time as any to peruse them. Besides, I needed to do something to get *me* out of the doldrums.

I grabbed a bottle of water and headed to my bedroom. When I reached the top of the stairs, I started at the sight of Corky coming down the hall. He stopped in his tracks when he saw me, and his face flushed.

I stood there and waited for him to come to me, my brows raised and my lips pressed together.

He swallowed hard. "Uh, I thought I'd check and see if any of the bathrooms needed towels or anything."

"That's not part of your job, Corky," I said. "In fact, you don't have any duties that would bring you upstairs."

"Sorry," he mumbled. "I was just trying to be helpful." He slipped by me, and I watched as he hurried down the stairs.

I stood tapping the newel post. Now what? Should I follow him and confront him again? Demand he tell me what he was really doing up here? But then, he wouldn't tell me if he was up to no good. And although I found it unlikely, he might have really been checking towels, just to be helpful. He'd been doing little extras lately, since I'd been so busy. Although, to my knowledge, he'd never come upstairs before. I wondered if Sheriff Turner had investigated Corky. Probably not. The sheriff seemed focused completely on the bank robbers. But what if Corky was involved with the bank robbery? Maybe he'd come to Cedar Chapel to case the place, and working here was a cover.

My head pounded as I walked to my room, so I went to the medicine cabinet in my bathroom and took a couple of aspirin. I came back into my bedroom and sank into the easy chair, closing my eyes. I didn't intend to sleep but woke suddenly with a start. Glancing at my watch, I saw that I'd slept almost an hour. Thankfully, my headache was gone. I stood and stretched the kinks out of my back. When I stepped out into the hallway, the house was still very quiet, so I assumed the boarders were all resting. Just to be sure, I went downstairs. Sure enough, no one was anywhere on the first floor except Corky, chopping vegetables in the kitchen. He glanced up as I peeked in and gave me a sick-looking smile. I nodded my head and turned away.

I went back to my room. Maybe I'd have time to read at least some of the letters. Sinking into the chair again, I removed the small bundle from the drawer and untied the blue ribbon. As the envelopes fell loose, a faint hint of lilac wafted from them, and as I picked up the first letter, it felt dry and almost brittle. No wonder. The first few letters in the stack were very old, dating back to the 1940s and early 1950s. Most of them were from young soldiers declaring their undying love to Aggie. One letter, in particular, caught my eye. It was from someone named Tyrone who lived in New York City. I remembered Aggie mentioning him in her diary before she fell for Frank.

June 15, 1943

Dear Agatha,

Just writing your name sends chills down my spine. Agatha. Agatha. If only I could speak that name to you in person. I can't tell you how much I miss you. The days are crawling by, and I don't know if I can wait until July when your family comes to the city.

There were two more pages of the juvenile drivel, and then he signed it *Your adoring and miserably lonely Tyrone.* Three more letters followed along the same lovesick line, and the last one from Tyrone was dated September of the same year.

Cruel, heartless Agatha,

No, I won't think of you that way. It's my own miserable fault you don't care for me anymore. It must be. Do you despise me because I'm not fighting? I would quit school and sign up, but Father would never allow it. But there I go again, trying to make excuses for not being worthy of you. I can't bear to know I'll never hold your soft hands in mine again, or touch your beautiful face. I've decided to end it all. You'll never be bothered by my presence again. When you hear my name next, it will be in the shocked tones of those who've heard of my death.

Yours through eternity,
Tyrone

Ah yes, this was one of the boys Aggie had mentioned in her diary. She had called him an idiot among other things and had written about the suicide threat—and then a little later that he was seeing someone named Hallie.

I chuckled and picked up the next letter, expecting more of the same. This one also had a New York City postmark. However, it didn't appear as old as the previous ones. I sat up, alert. The letter was from Forrest Pennington's son Simon, and it was postmarked 1986.

Dear Aunt Aggie,

Father passed away last week. We tried to reach you by phone, but never got an answer. We also wired you, but since we haven't heard back, I can only assume you didn't receive the telegram. Father spoke of you often in his last days and wanted to reconcile, but I'm sure you remember how stubborn he was. In spite of his desire to see you again, his pride held him back. I would like very much to meet you. After all, we are relatives and shouldn't be alienated like this. My wife and children are eager to know you, as well. You have my address and phone number now, so I hope you'll contact me.

Sincerely,
Simon Pennington

And another the same year.

Dear Aunt Aggie,

It was so wonderful to meet you. I can't tell you how much we enjoyed your visit. I hope there will be many more. The children miss you, and Dane is already talking about our planned get-together in Branson this summer. He's after me every day to make our reservations.

The letter continued, and several others, as well, about family matters. It seemed as though Miss Aggie had reunited with her brother's family, at least for a while.

Yawning, I reached for the next letter. The postmark revealed it to be from Jefferson City, Missouri, the year 1992.

Dear Aunt Aggie,

Just a short note to let you know we still love you and think of you often. The children still talk about you. I know you said in your letter you don't want to have any more contact with us, but I can't help but hope you've changed your mind. Charlene will graduate from high school this year. Dane is a freshman. Our little Lauren is eight years old now. She's getting very good at the piano and sings like an angel.

There were one or two more letters from Simon pleading for reconciliation or at least an explanation. I was curious to know why Miss Aggie broke off contact. I did know, however, the letters were too recent to ignore. I copied the address and phone number, then retied the ribbon around the letters. Not wanting to wake the seniors, I tiptoed down the hall to Miss Aggie's room and returned the diary and letters. I glanced around the darkened room. Did it hold a clue to Miss Aggie's whereabouts? Something we'd overlooked? Fear, like sinister fingers, crept up my spine. Shivering, I left the room and stood outside the door, arms clutched tightly around my chest, my heart pounding. After a few minutes, my nerves calmed down, and I silently laughed at myself. I really needed to stop giving in to my imagination so much.

I glanced at my watch. The seniors would probably rest for at least another half hour. Plenty of time to try the Pennington phone number. I went back to my bedroom, picked up the phone, and dialed. The phone rang several times then switched to an automatic voice mail message stating the mailbox was full. Disappointed, I hung up the receiver.

Muffled footsteps on the carpeted hall announced the boarders were up from their naps. I should probably go down and see if I could get them interested in a board game or two. Anything to prevent the return of the morning's gloom. I knew depression was sometimes common with elderly people, but these special friends of mine were usually cheerful and active. I didn't want the very real fact of Miss Aggie's disappearance to lead them downhill into despondency.

The games were a colossal failure. Frank and Martin bickered over every move, and Miss Evalina flat out refused to play. She sat in a corner chair, reading a magazine and interrupting the game every now and then to remark about something she'd read. Usually something political. And always something she disagreed with.

Finally, I gave up and decided to take a walk. I grabbed my coat and left the house, breathing deeply of the fresh, crisp air as I headed down the sidewalk. The sun was out and felt good through my coat. I was glad I hadn't worn the new, heavy one I'd recently purchased.

"Victoria. Yoo-hoo. Victoria." Glancing over my shoulder, I stopped when I saw our neighbor, Janis Miller, trudging down the sidewalk after me, her hands waving frantically.

"Hello, Mrs. Miller. Did you need something?"

"Oh, no." Her brown eyes sparkled, and her wrinkled face scrunched up as she gave me a friendly smile. Too friendly. "Saw you leaving and figured I could use the exercise, too."

She took hold of my arm and patted my gloved hand. Uh-oh. I was pretty sure she was after something. Or else had some gossip she wanted to pass along. I should have slipped out the back way. Not that I disliked Mrs. Miller. I'd known her most of my life. But unfortunately she'd been worming things out of me since I was a little girl. Usually things she didn't need to know. I'd been in trouble more times than I liked to remember for revealing personal family matters to the lady.

"That's nice, Mrs. Miller. Glad to have the company." Oh, what a liar I can be sometimes. *Forgive me, Lord.*

"I'm so sorry about Aggie, sweetie. I'm just worried to death, as I know you are, too."

"Yes, ma'am. It's really hard. Especially on her friends. Did you know her when you were growing up?"

"Oh, heavens no, child. I met Gerald in St. Louis.

But this was his hometown and he always wanted to come back. We moved here after his mother died and left us the house. That was long before you were ever thought of." She chuckled and patted my hand again. "About Aggie, now . . ."

Oh, boy, here it came. Whatever it was.

"I hear she'd been getting on the Internet, down at the library."

I stopped in my tracks, and she released my arm.

"Where did you hear that?"

"So, it's true?"

"I didn't say it's true. Who told you?" I hoped it wasn't anyone in our little band of detectives, but who else could it be? Louise wasn't about to admit she let Benjamin hack into the library computer.

Mrs. Miller bit her lip, as though she'd accidentally let the cat out of the bag.

"I'll tell you, but don't you be getting mad at her." She tipped her head coyly, and I closed my eyes. Oh, no. It *was* one of us.

"Georgina told me. But only because she was so worried."

"Oh!" I couldn't prevent the little exclamation of exasperation from leaving my lips.

"Now don't you be getting onto Georgina. I made her tell me." Well, I could easily believe that. "And it's a good thing I did," she added. "Because it was important information."

"But the files didn't turn up anything," I said. "It was nothing but a wild goose chase."

"Yes, I know that, Victoria. However, that's not the only computer in the world, you know."

"What other computer could Miss Aggie have used?" And then it dawned on me.

Mrs. Miller must have seen the realization on my face. "Umm-hmm," she said. "I'm surprised you haven't thought of it yourself."

"No. I can't believe Miss Aggie would use my computer without asking." But why not? Everything at the lodge, except for personal items which we kept in our bedrooms, was pretty much community property as far as the boarders and I were concerned. If Miss Aggie had wanted to use the computer, it wouldn't have occurred to her she should ask permission.

"Mrs. Miller, I appreciate your suggestion, but I very much doubt Miss Aggie used my computer. Even if she did, I'm sure it was for recipe searches or to check out hotels and restaurants. Just like at the library." I smiled, but she didn't smile back. I could tell she wasn't going to let this rest. Unless I got away from her in a hurry.

"Well, I should probably be getting back home. I didn't realize how late it is. Guess I'll have to walk twice as far tomorrow."

I left her standing there and headed back to the lodge. This new idea, disturbing as it was, could actually lead us to a clue about Miss Aggie's whereabouts.

I slipped into my office and began to search my

computer files. If Miss Aggie had been in here, she might have left some evidence. But after spending nearly a half hour examining the computer, I'd found nothing to indicate Miss Aggie had made use of it.

I leaned back in my chair and closed my eyes. It was extremely doubtful Miss Aggie would know how to cover her tracks, but just on the off chance, I knew I should probably call Benjamin and ask him to do a deeper search. But what if he wouldn't talk to me? I couldn't blame him. I'd been pretty hateful and rude.

The bell clanged, announcing dinner. I supposed I should go up and change but didn't want to be late.

Silence reigned once more at the dinner table. Until Miss Jane yelled.

"Who kicked me?"

"I'm sorry, Jane. It was an accident." Miss Georgina frowned then ducked her head and continued to eat her meal.

"Well, be more careful," Miss Jane snapped.

Suddenly Miss Georgina squinted at Miss Jane.

From between clenched teeth, she said, "I told you . . . I'm sorry."

I stared at Miss Georgina in surprise. I'd never, ever seen Miss Georgina speak roughly to anyone or seen such an angry expression on her face. I'd better do something.

"Uh . . . excuse me. I'm sorry to interrupt. I have a problem and could really use some help."

Five curious glances turned my way. *Okay, Victoria. Think fast.*

"Umm . . . you all know Buster is creating a great deal of havoc around the house. He keeps getting loose, and just this morning he tore up three towels." I hoped the look on my face was desperate enough. The dog truly had torn up three towels, but they were old ones I'd put down for him. "I don't see how we can keep him. But I've been thinking. Maybe he wasn't dropped off. Maybe he ran away or was stolen or something. I'd like to try to find his owners."

"Oh, dear. If you're right, someone may be just heartbroken at the loss of their pet." I felt a little bit guilty as Miss Georgina wrung her hands. But at least she wasn't angry anymore.

"What can we do?" Miss Jane piped up, patting Miss Georgina on the hand. Apparently, all was forgiven.

Okay, this shouldn't be too hard. We needed to get out of this house anyway.

"How about if we all take a little trip tomorrow? Back to wherever you found Buster. We could just knock every time we come to a house and ask if they've lost a dog or know who he belongs to." Yeah, that should work, as long as we all stayed together.

"You can count me out," said Frank. "I'm working at the store tomorrow."

"Count me out, too." Martin nodded, then nodded again for emphasis, and didn't bother to give a reason.

"How about you ladies?" I glanced from one to the other, and each one agreed to go.

"But I have to be back here early," said Miss Evalina. "You know I have my Bible study tomorrow."

"Oh, I thought we'd go right after breakfast. It shouldn't take more than a couple of hours."

With that settled and peace restored, I got up and began to clear the table. I took a stack of dishes into the kitchen then headed upstairs. I had decided to call Benjamin but didn't want any listeners.

Benjamin wasn't answering his office or home phones. I tried his cell phone number but got his voice mail. I hung up. It would be hard enough to apologize then ask for his help without him having a recording of it to use against me. *Oh! I'm doing it again. Why can't I stop being so suspicious?*

I decided to try Simon Pennington's house again, but no one answered there, either, and still no voice mail.

I went downstairs and headed to the kitchen to talk to Corky about the next day's menu. I stepped through the door and stopped short. Frank and Corky were standing at the basement door, talking heatedly. They looked up. Frank sent Corky a warning glance and nodded to me grimly as he left the room.

Well, this was an interesting turn of events. Maybe my suspicions of them weren't so far off after all. Could Frank and Corky both be involved with Miss Aggie's disappearance?

Georgina! Hang on to him." Miss Jane's shrill voice sliced through the frozen air. I was trying to get the van warmed up, intending to bring Buster out after the ladies were bundled up nice and cozy in the back seat. But here they were. Miss Georgina pulling on the new leash, and Miss Jane pushing from behind.

"Wait a minute. Let me get out and help." I reached for the handle just as Miss Georgina fell backward, dragging poor Buster on top of her. He crawled over the back of the seat and landed on the full rear seat, almost taking Miss Georgina with him.

I put my head in my hands and leaned against the steering wheel. This had been a mistake. The temperature had dropped again during the night, and it looked like it might start sleeting or snowing any minute.

Miss Jane scooted in next to Miss Georgina, who had righted herself, and they both began to buckle their seat belts.

"Miss Jane, you forgot to close the door."

"Oh, sorry." She reached over and pulled the door shut then snapped the seat belt buckle into place.

"Are you ladies sure you're up to this? It's awfully cold. We could wait for another day to search for Buster's owners."

"We're fine, Victoria. A little bit of cold air never hurt anybody."

Miss Georgina gave a nervous little laugh. "Well, but Jane. It is mighty cold. And those clouds don't look too good."

"Nonsense. Didn't you watch KY3 this morning? It's supposed to clear up by noon."

Reluctantly, I backed out of the driveway. I had turned onto Main, toward the supermarket end of town, with Miss Jane directing, when the sleet began pelting a staccato against the windshield.

"Oh, dear." Miss Georgina sounded frantic.

"Now, don't you start that, Georgina. Victoria knows how to drive. She's not going to kill you."

"Maybe we'd better pull over until it slacks up," I said. "It's coming down pretty fast, and the wipers are having a hard time keeping up."

I eased into a parking spot in front of Whitly's Body Shop and glanced nervously around. I should have known better than to come out, but I wasn't used to the weather here yet and hadn't realized how fast a storm could come on.

The door to the shop opened, and a bundled-up Junior Whitly hurried over to my door, holding his gloved hand in front of his face. I rolled down the window.

He looked at me as though I had a couple of screws loose. "Miss Storm, whatcha doin' out in this?"

Feeling like an idiot, I avoided his question and

threw him a quivery smile. "Do you think it's going to stop soon?"

"No, 'fraid not. I just now heard we're supposed to get six to eight inches of snow before morning."

Miss Georgina gasped and cast an indignant glance at Miss Jane.

"Well, I only know what Brandon said on KY3," Miss Jane said. "That's all I know. It's not my fault if he got it wrong." She glanced at Junior. "How have you been, Junior?"

"I'm fine, Miss Brody." He gave a nervous laugh. "If you're wonderin' where Taylor is, he's on vacation. Asked me to run the shop by myself for a while."

"Oh. Okay."

"But I'm going on vacation, too, tomorrow, so the shop'll be closed."

"Well, take care, Junior." Miss Jane had a decidedly confused look on her face.

Buster chose that moment to remind us of his presence with a mournful howl, nearly sending my frazzled nerves through the roof.

"Okay, Buster, calm down," I said. "We're going home."

I drove home as slowly as possible and pulled into the garage with a sigh of relief. We piled out and the ladies headed into the house, while I took Buster around to the basement door and wrestled him down the steps. I yanked my gloves off as I hurried up the stairs into the warm kitchen then leaned against the door, rubbing my hands.

"Coffee?" Corky stood holding the pot and my favorite coffee mug.

"Thanks, but you know what? I'd prefer tea. If you'll put on some water to boil, I'll go upstairs and change into some sweats and a sweatshirt. Then I'll be down to make it in a little bit."

I hurried to my room. After donning my warmest sweatpants and shirt, I ran a comb through my unruly hair and left my room. I'd just started down the stairs when I heard a door opening behind me and turned around to see who it was.

Miss Evalina stood in her doorway, her eyes red and puffy. She motioned me over.

"Do you need something?" I peered into her sad, watery blue eyes.

She stood up a little straighter. "If you have a minute, I'd like to speak to you."

"Of course. I was just going down to make some tea. Would you like some?"

"That would be lovely. I'll just leave my door open till you get back with the tray."

Ten minutes later I stepped into the inviting warmth of Miss Evalina's room and set the tray, with Grandma's best china teapot and cups, onto a small table in front of her sofa.

"Would you like to pour?" I asked, motioning toward the rose-covered teapot.

She nodded and proceeded. I would have loved to lean back against the soft brocade, but Miss

Evalina sat straight and proper, so I followed suit, inhaling the heady aroma of Earl Gray tea as we sipped the delicious brew.

We sat for a while and spoke pleasantly of the fine china, the weather, and a book we'd both recently read. Then when the pot was empty, Miss Evalina leaned back. I sighed and sank back into the luxuriously posh cushions, breathing in the soft fragrance of lavender wafting softly through the air.

"I'm ready to tell you the complete story of what happened with Aggie, Frank, and me."

I sat up in surprise, giving her my undivided attention.

"Sit back, Victoria. Relax. It's nothing earth-shattering. Just a typical story of three young people. A young woman who was used to getting what she wanted. A young man who was foolish and besotted by her charm. And another young woman who didn't have the gumption to fight for the man she loved. So she let him slip out of her life."

I sat and soaked it all in as Miss Evalina spoke of the friendship and love she'd shared with Frank Cordcll. Thc laughter, the tears, even the first kiss. As the story progressed, I felt I was right there watching the story unfold. I grew angry when Aggie made her play for the returning soldier, the love of Miss Evalina's life. But that sweet lady smiled sadly and patted my hand.

"Aggie wasn't much more than a child. She'd always been spoiled but was never satisfied. She could have had any young man she wanted, but Frank's resistance only kindled her determination. In the end, she may have suffered more than any of us."

I felt anger again as Frank told Evalina, with sorrow and apologies, that he loved Aggie.

Again, Miss Evalina shook her head and calmed me down. "Frank was just home from a horrible war. His emotions were still shattered from the things he'd seen in the concentration camps." She paused for a moment and something, pain perhaps, distorted her lovely face. "He'd never been pursued by someone such as Aggie, and I'm afraid it rather went to his head."

I cried when the young Evalina, with dry eyes, told him she understood, removed a heart-shaped diamond special cut for her from her finger, and sent him on his way.

"Don't cry, Victoria. It was a long time ago, and after all, I survived. When Mr. Pennington forbade Frank to see Aggie, he went away and sometime later married Betty. When he brought her back to Cedar Chapel, she and I became friends. I'm sure she knew about Frank and me. In a town of this size, she'd have to. But she never mentioned it and neither did I. Aggie went through a devastating period of her life. I told you some of it. But there was more. I don't know if she would have written about it in her diary or not. If she did, then you already know."

"You mean the falling out with her brother?"

Miss Evalina nodded. "It hurt her a lot."

"Didn't you ever fall in love again?"

Her eyes grew misty. "No, I never did. But I've been happy with my life. Teaching has been quite fulfilling, and I've been blessed with many friends, both old and new, who have been such a joy to me. Even Aggie and I became friends. She was such a little goose. She needed a friend to guide her and care about her." She frowned. "I thought I could keep her safe. But I was wrong."

"But whatever happened to Miss Aggie, it has nothing to do with you." And I really meant that.

"Thank you. I couldn't bear having you suspect me of harming Aggie."

"I don't think I ever really did. I've sort of been grasping at straws. Still am, to be honest. Forgive me if I was unkind."

"It's not your fault. I've behaved like an old grump lately, especially where Aggie and Frank are concerned. I don't know what's gotten into me."

I gave her a hug then gathered up the tea things and carried them downstairs, leaving her to compose herself.

After washing the tea service and putting it away, I found the other ladies seated side by side on one of the sofas in the front parlor. They looked up expectantly as I walked in and sat down in one of the wicker rockers.

"Eva told you, didn't she?"

"Yes, Miss Jane, she did."

"Hhmph. I'll bet she didn't tell you everything."

"Why would you think that, Miss Jane?"

"Because Eva is too kind. She can't bring herself to speak harshly about anyone. Even someone who behaved as badly as Aggie did."

"Aggie was very cruel to Eva," Miss Georgina said.

"All right, you two. It's obvious you're dying to tell me something. I probably shouldn't listen to gossip, but I need to know everything in case there is a tie-in with Miss Aggie's disappearance."

I settled back in the little rocking chair and waited.

Miss Jane glanced at Miss Georgina and gave a nod of encouragement. "You tell the first part, Georgina. You were there, with Eva."

"Yes, you're right, Jane. I do need to tell this part." Miss Georgina cleared her throat and spoke directly to me. "You see, I lived with Eva and her family for about three years. You didn't know that, did you?"

"No, ma'am, I didn't."

"My parents were both involved with the government during the war. Our war, I mean. World War II." Her eyes swam with unshed tears as she continued. "It was necessary for them to spend long hours at the office where they worked, and they thought I'd be lonely in a strange city, away from my friends. Besides, they were afraid I might find out, somehow, about the horrors going on in Europe at that time. Only the government had even an inkling of the Nazi atrocities. For me, except for Mama and Papa being away, the war was just fun and games. We girls used to go spend the night with friends in Springfield and go to the dances to entertain the boys getting ready to ship out." She blushed and dimpled. "Of course, our parents never knew."

I couldn't let her get off track. She'd get confused and never get back to the subject.

"So your parents left you with the Swaynes?"

"Oh, yes. Eva's father and my mother were second cousins and they'd been friends all their lives. It was only natural that I'd stay with them."

"So what happened with Miss Evalina and Frank that you don't think she told me?"

"Did she tell you she locked herself in her bedroom the night Frank broke up with her and didn't come out for nearly a week?"

I sat up straighter and shook my head.

"Why don't you tell me about it?"

"She was totally devastated," Miss Georgina said. "When Frank left that day, Eva went straight to her bedroom and refused to come out. Finally, on the third day, she let me bring her some food and water, but she only ate a few bites. I was shocked at her appearance. I was afraid she was dying. Her hair was uncombed, and her lips were dry and parched. I found out later the water in her pitcher had run out the day before." Miss Georgina licked her lips, and her brow furrowed with concern, as if she were reliving the events even as she spoke.

"She wouldn't talk, not even when I begged her to come down. After that, she let me in with a tray every day, but I don't think she ever ate more than a bite or two. I was the only one she'd allow in her room. And she wouldn't talk to me at all, until the last day." A strange expression crossed her face, and she swallowed hard. "She looked different that day. She'd been crying again, but she seemed so happy. To tell you the truth, at first I was afraid she'd lost her mind.

"She said I was not to speak badly about Frank Cordell or Aggie Pennington in her presence and to tell everyone we knew she wouldn't tolerate any criticism of them. Then she thanked me for being kind during her time of sorrow and said she was fine now and was coming down for dinner."

Miss Georgina looked at me with wide eyes. "And she did. And from that time on, we never mentioned the fact that Frank Cordell had been her very world since she was a small child."

She exhaled deeply and looked at Miss Jane. "You'd better tell her the rest, Jane. And don't worry. Everyone knows how much you love Eva."

Sorrow crossed Miss Jane's face. The look she

gave me could only be described as pleading as she spoke.

"You see, I was Aggie's best friend. I've always been Aggie's best friend. Even when I wanted to slap her sometimes. Even during the bad years, when she wouldn't have anything to do with me or anyone else. But back when we were in our teens, I'd go along with just about anything to get her approval."

It was hard for me to imagine Miss Jane being a follower of anyone.

She paused for a moment, lost in her memories, then continued. "The day after Frank broke up with Eva, I was at Aggie's house, and all she could talk about was Frank and their plans. I was shocked when she showed me the ring on her finger. I said, 'Aggie. That's Eva's ring.' She just laughed. She said Frank had planned to buy her a different ring, but she'd insisted on having that one. I think that was the first time I faced the fact that Aggie had a mean streak." A fit of coughing stopped her, and, concerned, I handed her a tissue while Miss Georgina pounded her on the back, none too gently.

"Rest a minute, Miss Jane. I'll go get us all some water." I hopped up and headed for the kitchen. Corky was nowhere in sight. I took three bottles of water from the refrigerator and went back to the parlor.

Miss Jane took a long drink and cleared her throat. "I'm all right now," she said. "Let me get on with this." She adjusted a cushion behind her back and leaned into it.

"As I said, this was the first time I'd seen Aggie's cruel streak, but unfortunately it wasn't the last. When Mr. Pennington refused to allow Aggie and Frank to see each other, she went on a total rampage. It seemed as though she couldn't find enough hateful ways to hurt Eva. She made a point to flash the ring in front of Eva's eyes every chance she got. She would be sure to tell someone about Frank's love for her every time Eva was in hearing range. And then, when Frank went away, she read his love letters aloud whenever we gathered together."

"But why did Miss Evalina put herself in that position? I would have avoided every place I knew Miss Aggie would be."

"Yes, but, Victoria," Miss Georgina said, "we were a close group of girls here in Cedar Chapel and the surrounding area. To avoid one was to avoid all."

"There was something else, though. Something I did." Miss Jane's eyes brimmed with tears.

"What was it, Miss Jane? I can't imagine you doing anything cruel to Miss Evalina."

"But I did. I did." She closed her eyes for a moment and hung her head. Then, raising tortured eyes, she continued with her confession. "At first I wouldn't do it. But Aggie convinced me if I was truly her friend, I'd help her. We wrote a letter to Eva, faking Frank's handwriting. In the letter, *he* told her he'd never loved her the way he loved Aggie. *He* said he'd always felt like she was a sister, but he didn't want to hurt her feelings, so he'd pretended to be in love with her. I sent the stamped, addressed letter to my cousin in Kansas City and asked her to mail it, saying it was a joke for someone."

She bit her lip and nodded at Georgina, who reached over and patted her on the shoulder.

"I don't think I've ever seen anyone's face turn as white as Eva's did when she got that letter." Miss Georgina picked up the story. "She looked like death. She went into her room for a couple of hours and when she came out, she was better. Then after a few days, she seemed her old self again."

"Remarkable," I said. "How in the world did she stay so strong? And at her young age. And she showed no sign of malice towards Aggie?"

"No. Not a speck. No one could believe it. They kept expecting her to fall to pieces and lash out at Aggie." An expression of awe crossed her face. "But I knew what her secret was. I knew what made her strong."

"What, Miss Georgina?" I waited, hardly wanting to breathe and spoil the moment.

"Why, Victoria. I should think you'd have figured it out. The same thing that kept you strong when you lost your young man. And the same thing that kept you from going to pieces when Caroline passed away." She smiled.

"You mean her faith?"

"I mean, dear, that at the end of that week when

Eva hid in her room all alone, she met Jesus. And He's been her strength ever since."

That night, when I went up to bed, I picked up my suspect list and marked across Miss Evalina's name until there was no sign of it at all.

10

Miss Jane was right. I don't know where Brandon got his information, but the snow never did appear. Not only that, the sleet stopped and the sky cleared. Who would have thought it?

We agreed that if the weather stayed nice we'd go on our dog-owner hunt on Monday since everyone had plans for Sunday afternoon. And this time Miss Evalina promised to go with us. I thought maybe we'd even do lunch out. Some place different. Like the new Japanese restaurant over in Caffee Springs.

Just as KY3-TV's Brandon had promised, on Monday morning I awoke to blue skies and sunshine streaming through the window. I sang in the shower and whistled as I nearly skipped down the stairs, inhaling the delicious aroma of Corky's homemade cinnamon rolls.

"A whistlin' woman and a crowin' hen always come to some bad end." Martin grinned up at me from the bottom of the staircase. Now I knew the day was going to be special. Martin didn't grace us with smiles and grins very often.

"No, no, Mr. Downey. This woman isn't standing still for anyone's ax today. I'm determined to try sushi before I die."

His face twisted in disgust, and I laughed as we walked to the dining room together.

After breakfast I took Buster out to the van. He wagged his tail and jumped in readily this time.

"Thank you," I breathed, glancing upward. "There, now, Buster. See how easy that was? No little ladies knocked over and no scratches on the seat. Good boy."

Buster flashed me a smile from the backseat.

The ladies came out, laughing about something. An almost overwhelming mix of honeysuckle and watermelon assailed my nostrils as Miss Georgina and Miss Jane crawled into the second seat. My nose and lips puckered in protest. I recognized the honeysuckle as one of Miss Georgina's favorite scents, so Miss Jane must be experimenting with watermelon cologne. Miss Evalina sat in the front passenger's seat and buckled up, while I walked around and got in.

"Corky said to remind you today is his afternoon off."

"Oh, that's right. I'll have to rustle up supper for us."

I breathed a prayer of thanks when I saw the streets were pretty clear. I wasn't sure what to expect from the country roads, but with the temperature warming up, I figured they wouldn't be too bad.

As we left town, we met Benjamin's car coming in. The wide grin he flashed my way reassured me. Apparently he'd forgiven my behavior. Or maybe he didn't really care anyway. I'd call him when we got back.

Following Miss Jane's directions, I pulled onto a recently blacktopped road. We'd gone a couple of miles when Miss Jane fluttered her hand excitedly. "Look, Eva. There's the road to the old Darcy place."

"Yes, Jane. It hasn't moved in the last sixty years that I know of."

"Well, you don't have to be sarcastic," Miss Jane huffed.

Miss Evalina flinched, and an expression of regret passed over her face. "I'm sorry. You're right. Guess I woke up on the wrong side of the bed today."

Miss Jane leaned forward and patted her on the shoulder.

"It's okay," she said. "Remember Anna's going-away party? Everyone from three counties was there."

I listened in delight as the three friends reminisced about Anna Darcy's party. Sometimes I think I was born "out of time," as they say. When I was a little girl, I used to play dress-up with the old dresses and hats in the lodge's enormous treasure-filled attic. And even as I grew older I loved to listen to Grandma and her friends talk about "the old days."

"Pull over somewhere along here, Victoria." Miss Georgina interrupted my thoughts, and I slowed and did as she said.

"We found Buster right along here. He was scooting under that barbed wire fence, and I was just sure he was going to cut himself."

"Okay," I said. "Let's drive on and keep an eye out for houses or roads that might lead to houses." I drove slowly along the road.

"There. There's a house right over there." Miss Jane pointed at a house off in the distance. "Does anyone know who lives there?"

A little farther on, I maneuvered the van around an ancient Burma-Shave sign and turned onto a narrow dirt road. As the van bumped along the ruts, I struggled to keep from sliding into the deep ditches on either side of the road. We pulled into a circular drive in front of the two-story white house, right behind a fairly new blue sedan. The house was old but boasted new white paint. Green shutters on the windows gave the house an inviting, homey look. I had intended to get out alone to question the occupants of the house, but my companions thought differently. We ascended the stairs to the wide front porch, with Buster dancing around our feet. I knocked on the door and waited. Footsteps sounded from inside, and the door opened to reveal a middle-aged woman with a kind face and a graying, stylish bob.

Peering through the still-locked screen door, she smiled at us warmly and perhaps with some concern.

"May I help you?"

"I'm Victoria Storm from Cedar Chapel. My friends and I are attempting to find this dog's owner." I reached down and rubbed Buster's shaggy head. "Have you, by any chance, seen him before?"

The lady glanced at Buster and smiled again. "No, I'm sorry. He doesn't look at all familiar to me. Where did you find him?"

"He was found on the road over there, running loose with a rope dangling from his neck."

"Hmmm. He could have come from anywhere. I'm sorry I can't be of help."

We thanked her and left. I glanced over my shoulder to check seat belts, expecting to find woebegone expressions, but instead each face seemed carefully composed. Okay. Maybe I was the only one who thought it would be a good idea to find Buster's owner.

The next house we came across turned out to be empty. We made several stops after that, not finding anyone who recognized Buster. After each "failure" the seniors grew more cheerful. Even Miss Evalina, who hadn't shown a lot of interest in our newly acquired nuisance.

As we started to leave a large farmhouse on the eighth road we'd driven down, a black and gray Siamese cat came around the corner of the house. Buster's ears perked up, and with a bark, off he sprinted.

"Buster! No, no, you come back here." Miss Georgina took off after Buster as the rest of us stood frozen. I couldn't believe Miss Georgina could move so fast. The cat screeched, Buster barked, and Miss Georgina hollered as they came around the front corner of the house. Suddenly, Miss Georgina's arms began to flail as her feet slipped out from under her, and down she went.

As the thud of her fall resounded in my ears, I shook myself out of my stupor and hurried to kneel beside her.

"Miss Georgina, are you all right?" I visually checked her for injuries.

"Georgina! Georgina!" Miss Jane ran up, holding her side and breathing with effort.

Miss Evalina stood nearby with a concerned look on her face. "Jane, get out of the way, and let Victoria take care of her."

"I'm okay," Miss Georgina said. "Just winded, I think. I must have hit an icy spot. Can you help me up, Victoria?"

At that moment the owner rushed out of the house. He helped me get Miss Georgina on her feet. She seemed fine, but we carefully helped her into the van. Miss Jane got in beside her.

"Don't forget Buster," Miss Georgina cried out.

While Miss Evalina got into the front passenger seat, I went to look for Buster. Neither he nor the cat were anywhere in sight, so I ran to the backyard. There sat Buster, licking blood from his haunch and growling intermittently at the cat that stood three feet away with arched back, snarls like a wildcat's emitting from her mouth.

"Um-hum," I said, grabbing his collar. "Serves you right. You shouldn't have gone after her like that."

I turned around and stopped short. In the distance, on a hill, a grove of cedars stood majestically green in the midst of the barren oaks and maples. I caught my breath. I never get used to Missouri's beauty. Over the tops of the trees, I could make out what appeared to be a rooftop. It had to be pretty high up for me to see it over the hill and trees. It must be Pennington House. I allowed myself a few seconds to soak up the view then tightened my grip on Buster's collar and hauled him back to the van. Or I should say he hauled me, nearly dragging me off my feet in his rush to get away from the cat. The coward.

"Oh, look, Jane, you can see Pennington House from here. Or, at least the roof." Miss Georgina was motioning up toward the top of the trees.

Miss Jane sighed. "Too bad it was allowed to deteriorate. It was in pretty bad shape the last time I drove up there."

"Poor Aggie. I'm still not quite sure why she abandoned it and let it go to ruin." Miss Evalina shook her head.

The ladies grew silent as we got back on the road. It was nearly one o'clock, and my stomach was making itself known again.

"What do you say we give up this venture and go eat lunch. I don't think we're going to find Buster's owners."

Relieved murmurs of assent met my suggestion, so I headed the van back to the main road. Fifteen minutes later we pulled up in front of Fuji Japanese Restaurant in Caffee Springs.

I reached to unsnap my seat belt then realized no one else had moved. Glancing around, I was surprised to see all three of the ladies staring straight ahead with expressions of panic on their faces.

"What's wrong?"

They sat silently looking at me.

"Oh. I take it you don't like Japanese food. Right?"

"Well, Victoria, dear, I'm sure I wouldn't know. But I hear they serve raw fish," Miss Jane said.

"And sit on the floor," Miss Georgina added.

"And besides that," said Miss Evalina, "we're not dressed properly for a formal luncheon."

I grinned as I looked at the three determined faces. We all burst out laughing as I started the car.

Ten minutes later we were led to a table at a local steak house. As we tromped through the wood chips scattered over the floor, I had to admit I was a little bit relieved. Sushi might be fun to try another time, but right now the aroma of broiled steak smelled wonderful.

It wasn't long before sizzling hot platters were placed on the table before us.

"Umm, yum. You ladies were right." I closed my eyes and breathed in the delicious aroma then sighed with pleasure as I savored my first bite.

After the server cleared our dishes off the table, we sat back with fresh drinks.

"Did anyone think Junior was a little bit odd yesterday?" Miss Jane appeared puzzled.

"What do you mean?" Georgina stared at her friend.

"Well, first of all, I've never known Taylor to allow him to run the body shop alone."

Miss Evalina's eyebrow went up. "Junior was running the place?"

"Yes, and he sounded strange, even for Junior."

"Hmmm. Well, who knows. I hope Taylor's not up to no good."

"I know he gave you a lot of trouble when he was in high school."

"Yes." Miss Evalina took a sip from her glass. "And worse still, he used to drag Junior into his mischief."

I was impatient to move on to the subject of Miss Aggie. We hadn't really talked much about her in the last few days. Maybe it was time I got some input from them. I'd known them long enough to know they each had their own storehouse of wisdom.

I sat up and folded my hands on the table. How should I begin? Frank was their friend, and I didn't know how they'd react to my suspicions. Especially Miss Evalina.

"I have something I need to talk to you about. It concerns Miss Aggie's diamonds, perhaps her disappearance, and maybe even the bank robbery."

They all leaned forward, Miss Jane and Miss Georgina's eyes bright with excitement and Miss Evalina's questioning.

I started at the beginning and told them about Frank and the pawn shop, then went on to mention my suspicions of Corky. When I spoke of Frank and Corky talking secretly in the kitchen, Miss Evalina's lips tightened, and a wary look crossed her face. When she spoke, I strained to hear. "What exactly are you saying?"

I inhaled deeply to get my courage up. "Miss Evalina, I think Frank may be trying to get rid of Miss Aggie's diamonds. He's involved with Corky, too. And for all I know, they may even be involved in the bank robbery."

Miss Jane's mouth flew open, and Miss Georgina's eyes looked like saucers.

"Why, Victoria Storm," Miss Georgina managed to gasp out. "Surely you can't be serious. Frank Cordell wouldn't hurt a fly. And besides, why would he be involved in a robbery? He doesn't need money."

"Georgina's absolutely right," Miss Jane said, giving me an indignant stare. "Frank still has half interest in the candy stores. He has all the money he could ever need."

I bit my lip. I should have known they would react this way. I glanced at Miss Evalina, who had said nothing more.

She reached over and patted my hand, and I felt the tremor in hers. "Sweetie, I know these incidents might look suspicious to you. But Frank Cordell would never harm anyone. And he'd never steal.

Even if he was flat broke and hungry on the street, he wouldn't do it. I know him. There's nothing you could tell me that would change my mind about that."

She took a deep breath and leaned back. "But Corky? His actions do seem rather suspicious."

When we got back to the van, Buster jumped on the seats and licked us as though we'd been gone a year. I handed Miss Georgina the bag of scraps we'd saved for him.

"Would you slip him one of these to hold him over until we get home?" I asked.

"All right," she said, yawning. I didn't blame her. I could use a little nap right now myself. I pulled out of the parking lot and headed toward the main highway. No sense in taking the back roads. We'd pretty much covered all the houses.

"Well, would you look at that?" Miss Jane said. "Look who's coming out of Fuji's."

I glanced over at the restaurant we were passing.

"Why, it's Phoebe Sullivan. And Corky." Miss Georgina no longer sounded sleepy.

"I can't say I'm surprised," Miss Jane said. "Not after the way they were goggling each other at the bank that day and later in the coffee shop."

I wasn't really surprised either, but now, with all my suspicions about him and with Phoebe working at the bank, their little flirtation suddenly took on a new significance.

"Stop gossiping, Jane," Miss Evalina said. "Can't a man take a lady out to lunch? After all, it is his afternoon off."

We pulled into the garage right after Frank and Martin as they returned from wherever they'd eaten their lunch.

It was too late for naps, so the ladies settled into the parlor with magazines and tea, while Frank and Martin went into the rec room to watch a John Wayne movie. I checked the refrigerator and found meat-loaf and potatoes ready to warm up and a crisp salad. An apple pie stood on a stand on the counter, I laughed to myself as I realized my inconsistency. Well, he still needed blessing, I reasoned. Even if he turned out to be a bank robber or kidnapper or worse.

I shoved that last thought away and went to the phone to call Benjamin.

A husky female voice answered. "*Cedar Chapel Gazette*. Rhonda speaking."

Rhonda? Who was Rhonda?

"Excuse me," I said stiffly. "Could I speak to Benjamin?"

"I'm sorry. Mr. Grant isn't in the office today."

"Well, when will he be?"

"He'll be out for the rest of the afternoon. Would you care to leave a message?" Was that a smidgen of satisfaction in her tone?

"No, thank you." I hung up and dialed Benjamin's cell phone. After four rings, it clicked then rang once.

"Cedar Chapel Gazette." The same voice. I wasn't about to give her the satisfaction of knowing I called again. I slammed the phone back into its

cradle. A moment later I groaned as I remembered caller ID.

I paced the floor. *What is the matter with me? So Benjamin has hired a secretary or receptionist or something. So what that he never had one before. He'd always said he didn't need one. His employees, Jory and Steve, always answered the phone when he was out.*

I wasted most of the afternoon wondering about the girl and trying to decide what to do about Frank Cordell, Corky, and Phoebe. I could call the sheriff, but after his reaction to me so far, I nixed that idea. After all, I didn't really have anything he would consider evidence.

I tried Ben's cell phone several times and finally gave up. By ten o'clock the parlor and rec room were empty. I went to the basement to check on Buster, and after taking him outside for a few minutes and filling his water bowl, I headed back upstairs. As I walked into the foyer, I saw Frank on the front porch talking to someone. I tiptoed closer to the door. It was Corky. They seemed to be arguing, but I couldn't hear what they were saying. Corky turned and stormed off the porch, and I ducked into the great room as Frank came back in and went upstairs.

Well, the ladies had almost convinced me I was imagining things about Frank, but now my suspicions rebounded stronger than ever. Those two were up to something. And I was pretty sure it wasn't anything good.

I'm walking the flo–oor over you."

Now why did that little ditty pop into my mind? I stopped pacing for a moment and let my mind process the words and the tune. Oh. Okay. I felt a bubble of laughter rising. That was a line from one of Grandpa's favorite old "hillbilly" songs, as he called them. I sure wished Grandpa was here now. It would be so comforting to crawl up next to him as I did when I was little, sink into the soft, cool leather of his deep chair, and bring all these problems to him. Or sit side by side with him on the porch swing as I did when I was a teenager. He'd always listened intently to what I had to say. Sometimes by the time I finished talking, I had my own solution to the problem. But if I still needed help, he nearly always led me to the answer.

A sigh welled up from deep inside me. Grandpa wasn't here now, and I'd have to figure this one out for myself. I walked the four paces over to my bed and sank onto the soft down comforter.

What was I going to do about Frank? He was like family, and I didn't want to believe he had anything to do with Miss Aggie's disappearance. But there had to be a reason for his actions lately. And so far, I hadn't come up with anything that pointed to his innocence. As for his not needing money, maybe it wasn't about money with him. All I could imagine was Frank and Corky conspiring together to swindle Miss Aggie out of her fortune. Maybe even going so far as to try to sell her diamonds. Should I notify the sheriff? My stomach churned with anxiety, since so far he'd been uncooperative and hadn't taken anything I'd said seriously. Miss Evalina's continuous insistence that Frank was innocent made my decision more difficult. I didn't want to upset her again. I decided to wait a little longer and just keep my eyes and ears open. Maybe it was time to do some snooping in someone else's bedroom. I wished for once that Corky lived in the house, but searching Frank's room would just have to do. A wave of guilt rose up at the thought, but I pushed it aside. This was something I felt had to be done. Now to find the right time when he was out of the house and the ladies weren't around. Especially Miss Evalina.

With my mind racing in a dozen directions, I decided to have a cup of hot chamomile tea. Not my favorite, but its calming effect might settle my thoughts a bit.

I went down to the kitchen and put the kettle on. While I waited for the water to boil, I decided this was as good a time as any to call Benjamin. I hoped he'd forgotten the details of our little trip to Branson and back. Especially the restaurant part.

He picked up on the second ring.

"Hi, Benjamin."

I heard a sharp intake of breath.

"Hi, Victoria."

Hi, Victoria? That was all he could say after I'd fought myself for days to get up the nerve to call? Then got someone who was probably his new girlfriend instead?

"Can I help you with something?"

Okay, that's better. A little impersonal, but, then, that's the way I wanted it. Right? And it made it easier for me to ask a favor.

"As a matter of fact, I was wondering if you could come over. I'd like to get your input on some things. That is, if you're not busy, of course."

"Nope. Not a thing on my schedule tonight. I'll be right over." *No hot date with Miss Whoever She Was?*

I replaced the phone, turned off the teakettle, and put on a pot of coffee. Benjamin liked his coffee, day or night.

Fifteen minutes later, coffee mugs in hand, we shivered on the front porch swing so we wouldn't wake anyone up.

I glanced at him and caught what appeared to be a very tender expression on his face. Must have been my imagination, though, because the next instant, his old, mocking grin claimed its usual place of residence as he sat there making no attempt to start a conversation. Well, maybe he was waiting for me. After all, I'd called him.

I cleared my throat. "The reason I asked you to come over . . ."

"Yes?"

"Well, Benjamin, to tell you the truth, I'm really worried."

At my serious tone, the mocking smile disappeared.

"You see, I know you don't think there was anything strange about Frank and the pawn shop, but there've been more incidents."

I filled him in on everything that had transpired with Frank and Corky. Then I explained my concern stemming from Phoebe and the bank.

"Hmm. I'll admit, things seem a little suspicious," he said, "especially with this Corky guy and Phoebe. Could there be any explanation for his being upstairs other than searching Aggie's room? He may have simply been checking towels, as he claimed."

"I know. But that's not part of his duties and he's never done it before. And with everything else that's going on, I can't help but wonder. And what about Frank? I don't want to think he's involved, but his strange behavior and association with Corky make me think they're involved in this together."

Benjamin frowned and shook his head. "I don't think so. I know him too well to believe that, Vickie." Somehow the sound of the nickname on his tongue didn't sound so mocking this time. In fact, it held a hint of affection.

"Do you remember when my mother left?"

The shadow of pain in his eyes told me the memory was more than fresh with Benjamin, even after all these years.

"Yes, of course I remember."

"That's when my dad hit the bottle so hard and ended up having to shut down the paper. If it hadn't been for Frank and Betty, I don't know what I'd have done. I spent more time at their place than at home. They fed me and clothed me for years—and did it in such a way that I never felt like a freeloader."

Why hadn't I known that? I knew Benjamin had spent a lot of time with the Cordells back then, but I guess his true situation hadn't sunk in.

"When I was old enough, Frank gave me a job at the candy store. Remember how I used to bring you chocolate sometimes?"

How in the world could I have forgotten that? "Oh, Benjamin. I do remember. You picked on me so much back then, I forgot the really sweet things you did."

He grinned. "Did it ever occur to you I had a big-time crush on you and didn't want you to find out?"

Warmth spread from my head to my toes. Benjamin had a crush on me? Really?

I opened my mouth to speak. To tell him I'd secretly felt the same way, but once more, thoughts of Alan intruded, and I smothered the impulse.

I breathed in deeply then let the air rush out in a loud whoosh.

"Well, no, Benjamin. It never did occur to me. I wish it had. Maybe your meanness wouldn't have hurt so much."

"Now, Vickie. I wasn't really mean."

"Well, that's easy for you to say." I blew away a strand of hair that had fallen over my eye. "But we've gotten off the subject. I know you care about Frank, and I understand. But if there's even a chance he's involved in Miss Aggie's disappearance, are you going to let your feelings stand in the way?"

The softness that had been on his face a moment ago was replaced by something else. Hurt? Disappointment? Whatever it was, it made me feel guilty.

"Okay. I'll keep my eyes on Frank for you. And if I see anything that makes me believe your suspicions might be true, I promise I won't allow my feelings to get in the way."

"Thank you," I said. But somehow I didn't feel at all pleased. It was time to change the subject. And I knew just which subject I wanted to discuss.

"I tried to call you all day, Benjamin. But some woman told me you were out of the office. Your cell phone kept switching over, too. Even after hours."

"Yeah, sorry about that. I was doing some research and didn't want to be disturbed. Then afterward, I forgot to switch off call forwarding until just before you called."

"Oh, I see." He still hadn't volunteered any

information about the woman. And I wasn't about to drop it.

"So, when did you hire a secretary?"

"What? Oh, you mean Rhonda? She's not my secretary."

I felt my face getting warm. Okay, I'd said enough. Benjamin apparently had a girlfriend.

I glanced over and saw him watching me, curiosity inscribed across his face. Suddenly the corners of his mouth began to twitch. So now he thought I cared he had a girlfriend?

"Rhonda's a friend I met in college. She's out of a job and living in Springfield with her parents right now. I needed someone to do some filler work at the paper part-time, so I hired her. She was working at the office today."

"Oh, well, your personal life isn't any of my business. Please don't think you have to explain anything to me."

"She's just a friend, Victoria. Nothing more." Benjamin's voice had deepened, and he spoke with such a serious tone that I looked at him in surprise. All humor was gone from his face. Instead, sincerity and tenderness softened his features.

I exhaled the air I didn't know I was holding in, and a smile started deep inside. I knew I wouldn't be able to keep it off my face, so I didn't try.

"Let's you and me be friends, Victoria. I hate it when you're mad at me."

Friends? With Benjamin? Yes, I could definitely live with that. But first I had to get something off my conscience.

"I'm sorry I was so rude the day we went to Branson. And a few other times lately. I don't know what makes me get so riled at you."

Slowly, he reached his hand toward me and traced his thumb down my cheekbone.

"I do," he said. Bending over, he kissed my cheek, and when he spoke, his voice was husky with emotion. "I'll see you tomorrow, okay?"

I nodded and watched him walk to his car and drive away. Shaken and a little stunned, I went up to bed.

I wasn't a bit surprised to wake up the next morning to sunshine streaming in my window and the sound of birdsong. I had dreamed about springtime and Benjamin. The birdsong, however, turned out to be someone whistling on the radio. I laughed and rolled over, hugging my pillow. Benjamin and I were friends. Who would have believed it?

I must have dozed back off, because the next thing I knew, I awoke to pounding on my door.

"Just a minute. I'm coming." I jumped out of bed, slipped on my robe, and opened my door a crack, surprised to see Martin standing there fidgeting from one foot to the other.

"Victoria, come see what's on TV. Hurry."

I yanked on a pair of jeans and a sweatshirt and hurried down the stairs. All the gang, including Corky, were there watching the news.

"Another bank's been robbed," Miss Georgina said. "Over in Caffee Springs. Can you believe it? And we were just there yesterday."

The robbery had occurred just before closing the previous night. The news report gave the barest of information. If they knew anything more, they weren't reporting it.

After I showered and ate breakfast, I headed for my office to work on accounts.

That afternoon, having warned all the residents, I waxed the great hall then went down to the basement. I folded towels and washcloths, daydreaming all the while. I'd expected Benjamin to call and battled disappointment that he hadn't. What if I'd misunderstood his tender actions of the night before? My face warmed at the thought of my romantic dreams. I was such an idiot. He'd probably offered nothing more than friendship and I'd read his gestures all wrong. Actually, friendship was what he'd said. Very clearly. *Let's be friends.* And of course, that's what I wanted, too. Still . . . the look in his eyes hadn't been the look of only friendship. And there was a new softness when he spoke to me. And the kiss? Maybe I wasn't such an idiot after all. But why didn't he call?

A mournful howl from the other side of the

basement caused me to jump, knocking over the basket of freshly folded towels.

"Buster!" I yelled. That dog's howls sounded like something out of a werewolf movie.

Muttering, I picked up the spilled laundry and stuffed it all back into the washer. What was I going to do with that dog? He was such a nuisance. I spun the dial and pulled it to start the machine then turned around and glared at Buster.

But there he sat, having gotten my attention, his tail wagging and that big smile on his face. Okay, okay. I'm not crazy. I know dogs don't really smile and grin. But I'll bet just about anyone who saw that look on Buster's face would call it a smile, too. And who could resist a grinning dog? I got a sudden idea.

"Fine, I'm going to take you to get your shots. Let's see if you're grinning then." He cocked his big old head to one side as though trying to figure out the meaning of my words.

It only took me a few minutes to wash my hands, run a brush through my hair, and put on a little lip gloss. Forty-five minutes later, Buster and I walked out the door of the pet shop. He wasn't quite as friendly as he'd been an hour earlier, but when we got to the car, I opened the bag of doggie treats I'd bought and held one out as a peace offering. So, after spending money for the shots, a new collar, and a few other doggy items, I figured I might as well face it.

Cedar Lodge now had a nonpaying, four-footed, shaggy boarder.

After a quick stop to pick up dry cleaning, I headed back home. I pulled into the drive and stopped before the garage door. Buster followed me to the front porch, and as we walked through the front door together, I almost expected to hear Grandma's voice raised in protest.

I hadn't been home more than ten minutes when Benjamin called.

His voice sounded excited as he asked if he could stop by for a few minutes.

I'd waited on the porch for less than ten minutes when he pulled up to the curb.

"Did you hear about the latest robbery?" he asked as he walked up the steps.

"We heard about it on the news this morning. They didn't say much." To tell the truth, I was a little miffed that he'd come over to talk about the robbery.

"I know. I happen to know the sheriff over there. He gave me a call this morning, and I'm on my way over there now." He took my hand and pulled me to his side. My heart turned to mush. Maybe I hadn't misread him after all.

"I'm not sure what time I'll be back," he said. "And I didn't want to let the day go by without seeing you."

I blushed and glanced at him quickly to make sure he wasn't teasing. His eyes were anything but teasing. And he was still holding my hand. I guessed I should probably say something, but I really just wanted to bask in the warmth of the feelings coursing through me.

I cleared my throat. "I'm glad you came by. I wanted to see you, too."

He smiled at me and brushed back a strand of hair that had fallen across my face.

"Wish I could stay, but I've got to get over there before someone else gets the scoop. I'd like to get the story out in tomorrow's paper."

He leaned toward me and I closed my eyes expectantly. When his lips grazed my cheek, I opened my eyes in disappointment to find him grinning at me.

"Oh, get out of here, Benjamin Grant."

He laughed and chucked me lightly under the chin. "I'm going to be out of town for a few days, doing some interviews. How about lunch Sunday, after church?"

I caught my breath. Did he mean he was going to church with me? Or did he just mean after *I'd* been to church?

"I'll have to come home after church to cook for the boarders. Corky's off on Sundays. But would you like to have lunch with us?" I held my breath.

"Sure. What time should I be here?" Okay, so apparently he didn't mean he'd go to church with me.

"We always eat around two on Sundays."

"Okay. See you then." He started to walk away then stopped. "Vickie, there's something you need to know about this latest robbery."

Surprised at the sudden seriousness of his tone, I looked at him questioningly and he told me the news.

It was pretty much the same story. Three gunmen. One guarding the door, one at the register, and one at the vault. Only this time, someone was dead.

The rest of the week was disappointingly uneventful. If the sheriff had any leads, he was keeping mum about it. I was about to give up on the Penningtons. I'd tried day and night with no success. It was now ten o'clock on Saturday night and I'd let the phone ring three times. Not wanting to deal with the irritating voice mail message again, I was about to hang up when someone answered.

"Hello." The breathless voice sounded youngish and female.

"Hello? Is this the Pennington residence?" I asked.

"Oh. Yes, it is. May I help you?"

"My name is Victoria Storm. I'm trying to reach Simon Pennington. May I speak to him please?" I tightened my hand on the receiver.

"Sorry, he's not here."

"Well, can you tell me when you expect him back? It's very important that I speak with him."

"I've no idea where he is or when he'll be home. Could be any minute or it might be next week. Mom is at a ladies' retreat somewhere, and I just came over to water the plants because Dad never remembers." She gave a tinkling little laugh that brought a smile to my lips, even while her words filled me with disappointment.

"Then you are . . . ?"

"Lauren Pennington. If you'd like I can take a message and leave it for my father. He's pretty sure to turn up sometime tonight. That is, unless he's on a business trip. Of course, he may just have run over to my aunt Susie's or something." She paused. "Who did you say you are?"

"Victoria Storm. I'm the owner of Cedar Lodge, a boardinghouse in Cedar Chapel. I have some important information for your father concerning his aunt. It's imperative that I get in touch with him."

"Oh! You must mean Aunt Aggie. Oh, dear. She isn't dead, is she?" The dismay in her voice endeared her to me at once. I decided to tell her what had happened.

"I pray she isn't, Lauren. But she's been missing for more than two weeks. I'd hoped your father had heard from her."

"No, I'm sure I'd know if he had. But what do you mean by 'missing'?"

"Just that. She left one morning to go to the library and never arrived there." Saying those words out loud, again, brought a crushing heaviness to my chest. Trembling, I sat on the bed.

"And you haven't heard anything from her?"

"I'm afraid not."

"Well, Dad needs to know about this. That's for sure. He's always cared about Aunt Aggie. I'll try his cell phone. If you don't hear from him tonight or tomorrow, call back. Here, let me give you my home phone number and my cell phone number, too, just in case."

We exchanged information, and I felt part of the weight lift off my shoulders. At least now Miss Aggie's family was involved.

The next morning, as I entered the sanctuary at Cedar Chapel Community Church, I scanned the crowd, hoping to see Benjamin. I felt a twinge of disappointment that he hadn't come. But negative feelings don't hang around long in my church. From the instant the band started up until Pastor Carl took his place behind the pulpit and opened his Bible, the presence of the Lord was so strong, there wasn't room for anything in my heart but worship.

"Be holy, because I am holy."

As Pastor Carl's words from 1 Peter 1:16 rang out strong through the sanctuary, I examined my own heart. I could remember the moment I'd first accepted Jesus as my Savior. But had my actions shown that salvation lately? I'd been downright snappy with the sheriff and his deputy. And my attitude toward Ben? Sure, I'd apologized to him for that last outburst, but I hadn't been completely honest with him. I knew I needed to tell him about Alan instead of allowing him to think he had done something to upset me.

As I allowed my heart and mind to kneel at my heavenly Father's feet, I gave all the bitterness, anger, hurt, and childishness to Him. And yes, the shame, too. Freedom sang in my spirit, and I could only thank Him for opening my eyes to my shortcomings.

I drove home with a light heart.

The seniors were all back from their own church services, except for Martin, who planned to spend the day with his son's family. The three ladies bustled around the dining room, setting the table with Grandma's best china and silverware. Miss Jane gave a final smoothing touch to a lace-trimmed placemat and looked up with a very coy smile.

"We thought you'd want to use the best settings with your young man coming," she said.

"My young man?" I raised my eyebrow at her, and she and Miss Georgina giggled.

"For goodness' sake. Leave the girl alone. Benjamin and Victoria have been friends for years." Miss Evalina attempted, and failed, to look disapproving, as her lips quivered at the corners. I knew a smile was about to win. "Now, don't you two embarrass them today."

"Yes, and we're still friends. Only, maybe we're better friends now than we were as kids." I grinned at them. "But don't any of you be getting ideas."

"Actually, we're better friends than we were a week ago. Don't you agree, Victoria?" I spun around and my face flamed. Benjamin leaned against the door frame, enjoyment written all over his face.

“Yes.” The word came out in a squeak, and if my face could have gotten hotter, it would have. I cleared my throat. “I should hope so. I wasn’t behaving much like a friend a week ago.”

After we’d eaten dinner and Benjamin had complimented me almost to the point of embarrassment about my pot roast, I shooed everyone out amid protests and did the cleanup alone. I needed a little time to think, anyway. I still wasn’t sure about Benjamin’s intentions. But if his actions were any indication, he wanted to take our relationship to another level. And I didn’t know exactly how I felt about that. Oh sure, I was attracted to him. No doubt about that. But I still had unresolved trust issues stemming from my past relationship. Besides, I didn’t have time for romance, with Miss Aggie’s fate so uncertain.

“So, what have you two been up to?” Miss Jane was asking Benjamin as I walked into the parlor. Oh, no. She wasn’t even being subtle.

“Whatever do you mean, Miss Jane?” Benjamin said with an oh-so-innocent glance in my direction.

“Okay, everyone. Listen up. This speculation has gone on long enough.” I noticed I had planted my hands on my hips, so I hastily lowered my arms to my side. I didn’t want to appear belligerent. After all, I was a changed woman, right?

Glancing around the room at each of the ladies, my gaze finally rested on Benjamin.

“Benjamin and I are friends. Considering the fact

that we've practically been enemies for years, I can see how you might be confused about our present relationship, but I assure you, it is friendship and nothing more." There. Let them chew on that. The problem was the shadow that crossed Benjamin's face. Before I had time to think of something to say that would soften my words, the phone rang.

"Cedar Lodge. This is Victoria Storm. May I help you?"

A deep and refined voice spoke into my ear.

"Miss Storm, this is Simon Pennington. My daughter told me the disturbing news about Aunt Aggie."

"Oh, Mr. Pennington. Thank you for returning my call. Would it be possible for me to meet with you to discuss the situation?"

"Yes, of course. I've been eager to speak with you as well."

"Would it be convenient for me to drive up there tomorrow?"

"Of course." He gave me the address, and I noticed it was the same one on the letters. "Have you had any word from Aunt Aggie at all?"

"I'm so sorry, sir. We haven't heard anything since I spoke with your daughter."

A heavy sigh from the other end of the line spoke more than words. Simon Pennington truly cared about his aunt.

The house was three stories, red brick, and exuded dignity and old money. I turned into the steeply inclined driveway and set my emergency brake before climbing out of my car.

The heavy door was intricately carved. As I waited for someone to answer the doorbell, I ran my hands over the ornate woodwork.

A sixtyish man opened the door. He invited me in, and I entered a wide foyer. The doors on either side were closed, but straight ahead, French doors opened into an area filled with antique furniture pieces and a faded oriental carpet that reeked of old wealth.

With a smile, Mr. Pennington directed me instead to the door on the left. This room, in stark contrast to what I'd seen of the other, was both warm and inviting. I sank into the deep, white cushions of the sofa. My host pulled a chair over and started to sit facing me, when a kettle whistled shrilly in the distance.

"Ah, the kettle. Would you care for tea, Miss Storm, or would you rather have something else? I have every flavored coffee and chocolate mix imaginable, thanks to my wife. She likes to keep a good stock here for when the children come home."

"Tea sounds wonderful," I said. "And please, call me Victoria."

"Thank you. I will," he said. "Please make yourself at home." A gracious smile creased his face as he left the room.

I glanced around. The furniture was comfortable,

but obviously not expensive at all. In fact, compared to the house itself and the room I'd seen off the foyer, it was modest enough to make me feel very much at home.

Mr. Pennington returned with a tea tray containing not only tea, but a small container with a mix of sugar packets, artificial sweeteners, and creamers. I wondered if he'd seen me appraising his room.

"I suppose you're curious about this room."

Oh dear. He *had* noticed.

"I didn't mean to be nosy," I said.

"It's quite all right. Only natural you'd wonder. Actually, the house belonged to my wife's family. Handed down to my wife after the death of her father a few years ago. The ornate and rather forbidding furniture in the room behind the French doors is what's left of my father's portion of the Pennington inheritance. The rest of the house reflects what you see here.

"Father wasn't much of a business man, I'm afraid. He lost most of his inheritance when I was just a boy and was never able to replenish it." He laughed, and I could sense there was no bitterness in his words as he continued.

"My wife and I, on the other hand, have worked very hard at our business, and we hope to leave a better legacy to our own children." He smiled at me, and I knew he wasn't offended.

"How many children do you have, if you don't mind my asking?" I was pretty sure I knew the answer to that, but it served as small talk.

He motioned toward a framed photo on a small table near the door. Just as I'd expected, there were two girls and a young boy standing by their seated parents. A typical studio family picture.

"Nice family," I commented. "And I think you have a charming home. I like this room much better than the other one."

"Thank you, my dear. As do I." He leaned back in his chair and took a sip of tea. "Now, I'd like to hear about Aunt Aggie. And please be careful not to leave anything out. Sometimes a new person on the scene can catch something others haven't."

I began with the morning Miss Aggie left the lodge and told him everything, including the fact she'd been browsing the Internet, and our search of her rooms.

He sat quietly, thinking for a moment. "And that's everything?"

"Well," I said reluctantly. I wasn't sure how he would take this. "I read Miss Aggie's diary and the few letters in her room. I hope you don't think that was wrong, but I'd hoped to find something that would give us a lead. So far, nothing has." I wasn't about to tell him my suspicions of Corky and Frank just yet.

"I appreciate your coming, Victoria. I'm sorry, I can't think of anything offhand that might help. Please keep me updated. I'd like to know even the smallest changes in the situation."

"Of course, Mr. Pennington." I rose, and we started toward the door. As we drew closer to the door, my glance fell upon the family picture on the little table, and I caught my breath.

I stopped and leaned closer to see the picture better. The boy was about twelve, with soft dusty red curls framing his face. The kind boys hate and little girls love. His eyes sparkled, and a Dennis the Menace grin lit his face. "This is your son?" I asked, and I felt my voice tremble.

"Yes," he said proudly. "My son, Dane. He's a master chef in Kansas City. Probably one of the youngest in the United States." He laughed and then added, "My wife and I always thought he'd end up as a stunt pilot or race car driver or something equally dangerous. Imagine our surprise and relief at his choice of career."

I managed to stay composed as I shook hands with Mr. Pennington and walked to my car. As I fumbled to insert the key in the ignition, drops of rain began to pelt the windshield. Great, just what I needed. Maybe I should get a hotel room instead of driving back in the rain. But the thought of the picture strengthened my resolve to get back to Cedar Chapel as soon as possible.

Could it be? Or was it only my imagination? I'd need to get a second opinion on this before I did anything rash. But I'd bet Grandma's china on the identity of the boy in the Pennington picture.

Whish, whish, whish, whish. Corky, Corky, Corky, Corky.

I blinked my eyes and glanced around. The back and forth of the windshield wipers, coupled with the headlights shining on the dark road, had almost put me to sleep. At least the temperature had stayed above freezing. If the rain had turned to ice, I would've been forced to stop for the night. Thankfully, I was only five miles from home.

Ten minutes later I pulled into the driveway and drove through the open garage doors. Breathing a sigh of relief, I stretched my neck and shoulder muscles. I hadn't realized how tension had clamped a hold on me while I drove.

Miss Evalina looked up from her embroidery as I walked into the parlor and eased onto the end of the sofa where she sat.

"Where is everyone?" I asked.

"I believe they're all in the recreation room. Jane and Georgina mentioned something about playing Yahtzee, and Frank and Martin are working on Frank's radio again."

I managed a tired grin. That old ham radio had been Frank's main interest for weeks until Miss Aggie disappeared. I was glad he'd returned to it. But on the other hand, maybe it showed his lack of concern. I shook my head. I couldn't seem to think straight lately where Frank was concerned.

"What about Corky?" I asked, shooting the words out.

"He's already gone home. Your dinner is in the refrigerator ready to be warmed."

I nodded and tried unsuccessfully to relax my trembling hands.

Miss Evalina's penetrating glance searched my face, and she placed her embroidery hoop on the seat cushion between us.

"What's wrong, dear?"

"I'm not sure. Maybe nothing. I need to think about it awhile."

"Very well." Apparently taking me at my word, she picked up her sewing again and resumed where she'd left off, occasionally darting a glance in my direction.

Grandpa always told me to think an idea through before I spoke or acted, but after fifteen minutes of silent fidgeting, my thinking processes were leaving a lot to be desired. So much for fancying myself another Tuppence. Although now that I thought about it, she often sought advice from one source or another. Good idea.

"Miss Evalina, I need to talk to you about something."

Once more, she laid down the pillowcase, which now sported a little blue flower on the edge.

As she gave me her full attention, I told

her about the framed photograph I'd seen at the Pennington home.

"And you think the boy is Corky?" Two little furrows appeared between her lovely, faded blue eyes. "But . . . if Corky is Dane Pennington and has deliberately kept his identity secret, that's very suspicious. It could mean he really did have something to do with Aggie's disappearance."

I nodded. "My thoughts exactly."

Her eyes bore into mine. "Well, there's only one thing to do."

"You don't mean call the sheriff, I hope?"

"Of course not," she said with a shake of her head. "We need to have more evidence before we do that. I propose we look through Aggie's photo albums. We only glanced through them before with no idea what or who we were looking for."

I jumped up. "Great idea. I should have thought of it myself. I know there are several albums on her closet shelf."

"Shall we go look now?" Miss Evalina's face was pink with excitement as she pushed up from the sofa. I knew the strain of inactivity had to be hard on all Miss Aggie's old friends.

"Sure, why not?" I hesitated then blurted, "Would you mind if we looked through Frank's room, too, while he's downstairs?"

She drew herself up, ramrod straight, and glared at me.

"Victoria Storm. I have told you repeatedly Frank

Cordell would never do anything to harm Aggie. Why do you persist in this unwarranted suspicion?"

"Sorry. I guess it's not a very good idea, anyway." *At least, until I can check it out by myself.*

We crept quietly up the stairs to Miss Aggie's room, not wanting the others to get involved at this point. After all, we weren't sure about Corky.

A faint floral scent clung to the room. A remnant of Miss Aggie's Chanel No 5. Why hadn't I ever thought it odd that Miss Aggie wore three-hundred-dollar-an-ounce perfume? Apparently the only indulgence she allowed herself. Well, as far as I knew. I resolved then and there to be more observant of the residents and the details of their lives.

Miss Evalina stood by the door as I walked to the closet and removed the stack of photo albums from the shelf. She closed the door softly behind us and we tiptoed to her room.

No expensive perfume in Miss Evalina's no-nonsense room. Instead, the calming scent of lavender wafted through the air. As we sat on the antique sofa, I couldn't help but think of the emotional atmosphere of the room the last time I sat here. Tonight we were all business. Miss Evalina handed me an album, and we began to search for pictures of a curly-headed boy with a mischievous grin whom I feared had grown into a kidnapper, or worse.

After fifteen or twenty minutes of browsing, I turned a page and there he was, staring up at me.

A little younger this time. But undoubtedly the same child.

"Here, Miss Aggie. This is him." I showed her the picture, and she leaned over and looked as I turned pages, revealing more pictures of Simon Pennington's family at different stages of their lives. The final picture in the album was identical to the one I'd seen that morning.

"It's Corky, isn't it?" I couldn't keep the excitement out of my voice as I stared down at the picture of the unruly-haired Dane Pennington.

"Well," Miss Evalina said, "it certainly could be him." She studied the picture closely from one angle, then another.

I sighed at the uncertain expression on her face. "Look, Miss Evalina, look at the hair and the shape of the chin." I held the picture closer to her.

"Please," she said, leaning back. "Get it away from my face. I didn't say it's not him. There is a resemblance. But Corky is at least thirty years old. It's difficult to know how he would have looked at twelve. I simply can't say with certainty."

"I know." I slipped the photo under the plastic film and closed the album. Miss Evalina patted my hand and looked on in sympathy as I stood up.

"Dear, if it's Corky, we'll find out. It doesn't end here."

I brightened. "You're right. No one can hide their identity once someone's caught on to them. I wish we could go to the police, but they won't take me seriously until I have some real evidence."

We replaced the albums in Miss Aggie's room and went downstairs. I could hear Corky humming and rattling around in the kitchen. I looked at Miss Evalina, who shrugged.

"I thought he went home," she said. "But maybe he just ran an errand."

I took a step toward the kitchen, and Miss Evalina laid her hand on my arm and shook her head. She was right. A confrontation at this time, without evidence, would just tip him off and he'd be out of here. Then we might never find Miss Aggie. But I decided I'd have a talk with him the next day. I'd be subtle. And perhaps he'd reveal something without direct questions.

After I ate my dinner, which Corky warmed for me, he cleaned up and left. I put my coat on and took Buster outside. The rain had stopped, so I headed up the sidewalk. We could both use the exercise. As I passed the house next door, curtains fluttered in the front window, and I saw Mrs. Miller's face peering out. A squirrel scampered across the sidewalk ahead of us, and Buster barked and strained against his collar, dragging me along so fast I almost had to run to keep up.

"Slow down, you mangy mutt. Why I ever decided to keep you, I don't know." I jerked on the leash, and Buster sat on the pavement in front of me, casting a reproachful look in my direction. I grinned and patted him on the head. "Okay, sport, you can't have the squirrel, but there's no reason you can't go for a run."

I darted around him, and he jumped up and raced after me, overtaking and once more nearly yanking me off my feet. By the time we circled the block and ran onto the porch, we were both huffing, and I bent over to catch my breath.

A noise from the end of the porch startled me, and I saw Martin sitting on the swing, sneering at us.

"Thought you hated that old dog."

"I never said I hated him. Just that he's a nuisance. Which he is."

"He's more than that. He tears up everything he gets a hold of," Martin complained. "He tore up my February Classic Movie Channel Guide yesterday. And I hadn't even had a chance to look at it."

"I'm sorry, Mr. Downey. Can you get another one?"

"Nope, by the time they'd send it, February'd be over. Hhmph. March would be over."

"Well, I'm sorry. I'll try to keep him out of the rec room from now on."

After noticing mud on Buster's paws, I led him off the porch and around to the back.

"You'd better stay in the basement until I can get you cleaned up. Wouldn't want you ruining the floors."

I filled his water bowl and went upstairs.

As I stepped into the kitchen, a screech reverberated through the house.

• • •

I rushed into the parlor, tripping over someone's umbrella. Miss Evalina stood over Miss Georgina, rubbing the lady's plump hands vigorously to no avail. Miss Jane grabbed a glass of water from the side table and flung it at Miss Georgina.

"Miss Jane! NO!" I cried, too late.

Miss Georgina sat up with a gasp, her curls soaked and plastered to her head, while the lace on her blouse lay limp and soaked.

"What were you screeching about?" Miss Jane asked.

"Why did you throw water on me?" Miss Georgina choked out.

"Ladies, please," I said. "Can someone tell me what's going on here?"

"Georgina let out a scream to shame a banshee and passed right out," Miss Jane said, looking a little sheepish.

Miss Georgina trembled. "I saw someone looking in the front window."

I hurried to the front door and yanked it open. Mrs. Miller stood there with her hand raised to knock.

"Oh," she said, stepping back.

"Were you looking in the window a few minutes ago?" I blurted.

"Excuse me?" Even in the dim light of the porch I could see the guilt on her face, but she wasn't about to admit it, I was sure.

"Never mind. Come on in."

"Well, I never," she said, glaring at me as she stepped in.

In the few minutes I'd stood at the door with Mrs. Miller, someone had returned the umbrella to its stand and wiped up the water. Miss Georgina sat trembling or shivering, I wasn't sure which.

"For heaven's sake, Georgina. Go change into dry clothing," Miss Evalina scolded.

Miss Georgina seemed on the verge of tears. She bit her lip. "I don't want to go up there by myself. Maybe someone's in the house."

"Oh, don't be ridiculous, Georgina. I was the one you saw at the window." Mrs. Miller had the grace to blush as she glanced at me. At least she placed Miss Georgina's emotional well-being before her own pride.

"I just happened to glance in as I walked to the front door." She shot me a look that dared me to challenge her statement. *Hmmm. I guess you climbed onto the porch from the side.*

"Ah, that explains it," I said. Might as well go along with her for Miss Georgina's sake.

"Oh, I do feel silly, then." Miss Georgina relaxed visibly. "I'll just go on up and change my blouse."

Suddenly I remembered Martin hadn't bccn on the porch when I let Mrs. Miller in.

"Did Martin come in a few minutes ago?"

"I didn't see him," Miss Jane said, and Miss Evalina shook her head.

"Where's Frank?"

"He went up to his room right after you left with Buster." She frowned at me. "Why?"

"Oh, just wondered. I thought maybe Frank and Martin went somewhere together."

Mrs. Miller snorted. "You don't need to worry about that old jailbird," she said.

"What? A jailbird? Frank's been in jail?"

"No, not Frank. Martin." She tossed me a look that accused me of idiocy. "Do you mean to tell me you didn't know one of your tenants has a criminal record?"

I opened my mouth to ask for more information, but at the eager look on her face, I changed my mind. "Mrs. Miller, I'm sure my grandmother wouldn't have rented to someone with questionable morals."

"Well, maybe naivety overcame her common sense where old friends were concerned," the lady said with a sniff.

By God's grace I managed to hold my tongue. Miss Evalina didn't.

"Janis Miller, that's about enough of your mouth. You know the situation with Martin as well as I do. Do you need something or did you just come over to stir up trouble?"

"Well, Eva Swayne. I came over to be neighborly, but if that's how you feel I'll go home."

"That's exactly how I feel. Now if you'll excuse us, today's been a very trying day."

Mrs. Miller got up in a huff, and I handed her

coat to her with a little flourish as she marched stiffly out the door. Grandma would have forgiven me. I think.

I returned to the parlor and flopped down in the wing chair. "Does someone want to tell me what she was talking about?"

"You don't need to raise your voice." Miss Evalina sent me a disapproving look. "No one deliberately hid anything from you."

I've no idea why I felt like I was the one in the wrong. "Okay. So what is it that wasn't hidden from me?"

"Well . . . ," Miss Georgina spoke timidly.

"Don't tell her. She'll just get suspicious of Martin."

"I think she's already suspicious, Jane." I silently applauded. This was the second time recently that Miss Georgina had stood up for herself.

I glanced at Miss Evalina. Exasperation crossed her face as she sighed and lowered the pillowcase to her lap.

"Would someone please simply tell me why Martin was in jail?"

"Well," Miss Evalina began.

"It wasn't really jail at all," Miss Georgina interrupted. "He spent time in the penitentiary for robbing a bank."

"Georgina!" Miss Jane stomped her tiny foot.

"Well, it was just a little bitty bank robbery."

My stomach churned. A little bitty bank

robbery. And no one thought it important enough to mention.

"Miss Evalina. Why didn't you tell me? Martin may be involved in this crime. Maybe he's the ringleader. The brains behind it all. And Miss Aggie is your friend. I don't understand."

A pained look crossed her face. "Don't be ridiculous. Martin's crime occurred long ago. He was very young and foolish, and he paid his debt with ten years in prison. He's lived a respectable and honest life ever since."

"But . . . how do you know? Maybe he's just been fooling everyone."

She sighed. "This is the very reason I didn't mention it. I knew you'd react this way. And I also know Martin had nothing to do with Aggie's disappearance, or the robbery of our bank."

"But . . . how?" I asked again.

"It's a matter of trust. I've known him many years. I knew him and his family before the crime, and I knew the situation that drove him to think he had to do what he did. And I don't care to discuss this matter further with you."

"Well, I don't mean any disrespect to you, Miss Evalina, but I'm reporting this to the sheriff."

Miss Evalina shook her head and gave me a sad smile. "Don't you think he already knows?"

Maybe he did and maybe he didn't. I figured he'd probably ignore anything I told him, though.

I should have waited until the next morning instead of calling the sheriff at home. Interrupting his dinner didn't help his mood. After a few words, which I can only describe as sarcastic and mean, he informed me he already had that information.

That sealed it. Any faith I'd had in the sheriff's department evaporated with his attitude. I added Martin to my investigation list with Frank and Corky, since it seemed the sheriff wouldn't perform his job.

I dragged myself up the stairs and almost fell asleep in the shower. For the second night in a row, I went to bed without a time of prayer and Bible reading. I didn't even think to tell the Lord good night.

I sat sideways on the cushioned window seat in the third-floor sitting room, gazing out at the rain pouring in colorless sheets from dark gray clouds. A hot mug warmed my hands. I used to love stormy days. I'd curl up in the deep, soft leather chair in Grandpa's third-floor library and snuggle up in one of Grandma's afghans, with a mug of hot chocolate on the side table and a stack of Nancy Drew books on the floor. Later on, the stack changed to Agatha Christie, John Dickson Carr, and many other friends.

My steamy mug now emitted the fragrance of Earl Grey tea, but no mystery book could match the suspense going on at the lodge.

I sighed and wished I could turn back time. To be that little girl again. Or even the eager, bright-eyed teenager. If only Grandpa and Grandma could tell me what to do. If only Dad or Mom . . . I felt tears sting my eyes, and angrily I wiped them away. No time for that now. Dad and Mom had never been there for me and never would be. I stood up, pushing the thought aside.

I sneezed and wrinkled my nose. The third floor had been closed off when Grandma opened the boardinghouse. That kept the heating and cooling costs down, and she didn't really need the extra rooms. The rooms were in need of a good cleaning, though. Lately, I'd thought of opening up this floor and taking in more boarders. I could use the extra income. But I hated to lose the warm, cozy atmosphere of the lodge. The seniors were more like family than boarders. Who knew how it would change with outsiders living here?

I shoved the thought away and drained my tea mug then stood up, brushing dust off my slacks. Beneath the mounds of white-draped furniture, I could make out the shape of Grandma's rocking chair, the hutch against the far wall, and the chintz settee in front of the empty fireplace. Another fit of sneezing drove me from the room. I went down the narrow, carpeted stairs and locked the door behind me. Memories were sweet, but they'd keep for another day.

As I started down the hall, Miss Jane stepped from her room. She saw me and stared.

"You have cobwebs hanging from your hair," she said with a giggle.

"Oh my goodness," I said, pulling strands of the stuff from my hair. "It's worse than I realized. I'm going to have to find time to do some cleaning up there."

"You might as well wait a couple of months, until you have your spring cleaning crew in."

"You may be right. I'd hate to tackle the job alone." I took a final swipe at my hair. "Are the cobwebs gone?"

"I think so. Just a little teeny one here. Let me." She flicked a finger behind my ear. "There, that's got it." She gave me a grin.

I smiled back and on impulse said, "How would you like to go for a drive?"

A startled look crossed her face. "In this weather?"

"Sure. Why not?"

Her eyes brightened. "Why not, indeed? I'd love to go for a drive. Where are we going?"

"I'm not sure. Let's just get out of here for a while."

We walked down the stairs and grabbed jackets from the coatrack in the hall and umbrellas from the stand then headed toward the kitchen. We could hear Corky in the pantry as we passed through to the garage.

"Can we take my car?" Miss Jane looked longingly at the shiny black Cadillac parked behind Frank's truck.

I'd probably regret this later, but . . . "Sure. I'd love to ride in your snazzy Caddy."

By the time she backed the streamlined monstrosity out of the driveway, we were grinning like a couple of ten-year-old conspirators. Automatically, she headed toward the square.

"Okay, Miss Jane. What do you feel like today? A tea-drinking gentlewoman? Or a dangerous slinky sleuth?"

"Oh." She released the steering wheel and clapped her hands. Just as the car started to veer to the side, she grabbed the wheel. "Let's be sleuths. How?"

I gulped and inhaled deeply. "Well, let's see. For a start, we could bug Sheriff Turner, I guess."

"Wonderful. Let's go bug him. Maybe we'll wear him down and he'll tell us something."

She twisted the steering wheel and careened around the corner. I held onto my seat, laughing like a hyena and reaping frowns from the few people we passed.

To my surprise and vast relief, Miss Jane parked the car smoothly in one of the diagonal parking spots in front of the courthouse.

Tom stood guard again, in the guise of doing clerical work. He groaned when he saw us come though the doors, our raincoats and hats dripping on the floor.

Before I could open my mouth, he held up his hand.

"Don't ask. I'll tell him. Just wait here."

I heard a roar from the direction of the sheriff's office.

"What? Again? Tell her I can't see her."

By this time, I'd shoved past Tom and into the office, with Miss Jane following closely behind.

"Hi, Sheriff," I said, grinning.

He groaned. "The bane of my existence."

"Why, how nice," I said.

"Nice? You think it's nice I called you the bane of my existence?"

"Oh, that. It's okay. I'm not offended." I pulled out a chair for Miss Jane and sat beside her. "No, I meant how nice you seem to know the meaning of the word." *Oops, sorry, Lord.* "Sorry, Sheriff. That wasn't nice."

As they say, if looks could kill, I'd be dead. Sheriff Turner turned to Miss Jane and forced a smile.

"How are you today, Miss Brody? You really should watch the company you keep."

"Now, Bob, don't be rude. Victoria is simply worried about Aggie, as we all are." She gave him a pointed look. "You are worried about Aggie, aren't you, Bobby?"

I locked my lips and tried not to laugh as "Bobby's" face turned from pink to red to purple.

"Of course. Now, how can I help you ladies today?" he asked through clenched teeth.

"Oh, we just wanted to know how the case was coming along, since we haven't heard much from you." Miss Jane had done so well this far; I decided to let her handle it. "You promised to keep us informed, Bobby. Remember?"

He closed his eyes and took a deep breath. Opening his eyes, he looked at Miss Jane and spoke quietly. "Yes, of course I remember. But you see, I don't have anything to share with you at this time."

Okay, my turn. "You mean you have nothing you *choose* to share with us. But, Sheriff, I have some things to share with you."

He groaned and leaned back in his chair, listening silently as I told him all I suspected about Frank and Corky.

"Miss Storm, that's very interesting. Thank you for sharing your valuable input. Now, I'm very busy. If you really want to help Mrs. Brown, I suggest you go home and let me do my job."

He stood and looked at us pointedly, apparently not believing a word I'd said. We left without another word, and I could almost feel the door hit us as we scampered out.

"Okay," I said as we stepped onto the sidewalk. "That went about as expected."

"At least the rain stopped."

I grinned at her. Good sport.

"What next?"

I laughed. "I think we may be kindred spirits."

"Like in *Anne of Green Gables*?"

"Absolutely." I patted her shoulder and glanced around. "Let's try the bank again. We haven't checked there in a while."

"Good idea. We never did speak to Harley."

My mouth dropped open. She was right. Somehow, in the confusion, we hadn't talked to the president of the bank. Harley Porter, the one who'd been forced to open the vault to the second gunman. How could we have neglected to question him? *You're not much of a sleuth, Victoria Storm. Now get in there and take charge.*

Mr. Porter was in and willing to talk to us. Of course, he didn't know what we wanted to talk about. He motioned us to two padded armchairs in front of his desk.

"Now, Miss Storm, Miss Brody, what may I do for you today?" He seated himself behind a massive oak desk with the assurance of one born to lead. Hmmm. That might help us, since the officers probably hadn't intimidated him.

Miss Jane had done well with the sheriff, even though we didn't get any information out of him, so I glanced at her and nodded. After all, if nothing else, she could get a good rise out of another upstanding citizen who'd been a kid when she'd taught sixth-grade science in her heyday.

Miss Jane smiled sweetly at the bank president. "Well, Harley. We wondered if you could give us any information about the bank robbers."

"I see." He drummed his fingers on the desk for a moment. "I think I've told the sheriff everything I know. Perhaps you should ask him."

"Well, I would do that, except he's determined not to tell us anything. You know Aggie and I are lifelong friends, and the worry is just about to get to me." She put a hand on her heart and closed her eyes.

Concern flashed on Mr. Porter's face; then Miss Jane opened one eye, and he grinned. Hastily she shut the eye.

"It won't work, Miss Brody. You're trying to manipulate me."

Miss Jane sighed. "You're absolutely right,

Harley. Forgive me. And I understand why you don't want to go against the sheriff. He's a mighty powerful man around Cedar Chapel."

Mr. Porter's face turned red and his eyes squinted. "I'm not afraid of Bob Turner. And there wasn't anything important anyway. I'm sure you've read the newspaper account of the robbers' height, weight, and what they were wearing. The only thing I didn't tell Benjamin was that two of the men seemed a little familiar. That's all."

I watched, amazed, as Miss Jane reached over and patted his hand, a very satisfied look on her face. "How did they seem familiar, Harley?" she crooned.

He darted a suspicious glance her way, and if anything, the red of his face got deeper. Rising from his chair, he stared at Miss Jane and then suddenly burst out laughing. "Miss Brody, shame on you. You tricked me."

"Who, me?" Miss Jane looked the epitome of injured innocence.

Mr. Porter looked at her with admiration and chuckled. "Okay, you two. I've got work to do, and I don't know anything more than you do. But I'm glad I told you about the robbers. I've no idea who they were, but there was something about them. I wish I could figure it out."

We thanked him and left his office, with an eye out for Phoebe. We didn't see her, so we left the bank.

A few minutes later, we sat at the coffee shop drinking lattes.

"Miss Jane, I can't believe you. You had him wrapped around your little finger."

"Aw, I've known Harley since he sucked his thumb. Come to think of it, that wasn't so long ago." We both broke out in giggles.

"I like this sleuthing," Miss Jane said, wiping foam from her lip. "What other mischief can we get into today?"

"Hmm. I don't know. I'm too busy wondering about the robbers that seemed familiar to Mr. Porter. I wish Phoebe had been there so we could ask her about it." I took a long drink from my latte and hastily wiped my mouth with a paper napkin.

"Maybe you could invite her to dinner."

"Now that's an idea. Better still, why not have Corky invite her over for lunch tomorrow?"

"Good idea." She leaned back against the back of the booth.

"Are you tired? Should we head back to the lodge?"

"I am a little tired. But I'm not ready to give up the adventure yet." A look of sheer enjoyment crossed her face. "We could go question Louise some more."

"I don't know. She gets a frightened look on her face every time she sees me."

"Come to think of it, she sort of avoided me at church last Sunday." A look of regret washed over her face, but in the next instant her chin grew firm with determination. “But we can’t let anything keep us from a possible lead to Aggie.”

“I know. I agree. Even if we make the whole town mad at us.” I pulled some bills from my purse and left them on the table. Outside, the temperature had dropped and rain was falling again. Raindrops pelted us, so we agreed this wasn’t a good day to visit the librarian.

We opened our umbrellas and almost ran to the car. By the time we got back to the lodge, the rain was falling in freezing sheets. Benjamin’s car was parked by the curb.

Miss Jane pulled into the garage, and we hurried inside, shivering.

“Hello, ladies. Got a little bit wet, I see.” Benjamin sat at the kitchen table drinking coffee while Corky stirred a pot of chili. The aroma just about made me swoon.

Miss Jane and I hung our dripping coats on hooks inside the kitchen door. She excused herself and headed upstairs, while I dropped into a chair across the table from Benjamin.

“What have you two been up to?” he asked.

“Why? What makes you think we’ve been up to anything?”

He raised his eyebrows. “I was only making conversation, but your reaction to a simple question leads me to conclude you really *have* been up to something.”

I grinned. "Spoken like a true newspaper man."

"Okay. What's up?"

I glanced at Corky, who had stopped stirring.

"Nothing. Let's go to my office. That is, if you've finished your coffee."

He tipped the cup up, draining it. "I have now," he said.

We went to my office, and I closed the door, holding my finger up to my lips. I crossed the room and turned the CD player on, then motioned him over.

"Victoria, you're starting to worry me. What's going on?"

"Shhh. I don't want Corky to hear." In a whisper, I told Benjamin what Mr. Porter had said about the robbers seeming familiar. "Did you know about it already, Benjamin?"

"No," he muttered. "Sheriff Turner kept that little piece of news from me. Maybe I should talk to Porter."

He looked at me. "Stop wringing your hands." His smile softened his words. "You look like Miss Georgina."

Sure enough, I was wringing my hands. "I don't know what to do, Benjamin. It's been nearly three weeks since Miss Aggie disappeared. The seniors are getting frantic. What can I do?"

He looked at me in silence for a moment, and a strange look crossed his face.

"What? What are you thinking?"

"Vickie, have you thought of trusting God?"

I stared. "I thought you weren't sure about God."

He hesitated. "Well, this isn't about me. You're the one who said God will get you through anything."

"You're right, Benjamin. Thank you for reminding me. I'm ashamed you had to."

"Why? You're only human." He chucked me under the chin. "Even you can't be perfect every minute."

"Oh, you." I laughed, and he grabbed me in a hug.

"I'm going over to the bank to see if I can stir Porter's memory a little more. If you need me, call my cell phone." With that, he slipped out the door.

I headed up to my room to change. The hems of my jeans were wet from slopping through rain earlier.

When I'd changed my clothes and come back down, everyone had gathered in the dining room, where Corky dished up steaming bowls of his wonderful chili. A platter of sandwiches sat on the table.

"Victoria, who do you want to ask the blessing?" Miss Georgina's eyes looked longingly at the bowl in front of her.

"Oh, I'm sorry. Miss Georgina, would you, please?"

"Heavenly Father, we thank You for this food and ask You to bless it and the hands that prepared it. In Jesus' name. Amen." Amen. Short and to the point.

Something about a cold, stormy day makes chili the best food in the world.

I tried to follow the conversation as we ate, but my mind wandered back over the events of the day. Who were the robbers? If they were familiar to the bank president, did that indicate they were locals? If so, why didn't Phoebe mention it? Perhaps because she's involved with Corky and Corky's in cahoots with the robbers?

That night I took out my suspect list and added another name: *Phoebe Sullivan: As a bank employee, could she be involved in the robbery somehow?*

I chewed on the end of my pen for a few minutes until I remembered the ladies' discussion at lunch a couple of days earlier.

Junior Whitly: Because Miss Jane thinks he was behaving strangely.

Taylor Whitly: Because the ladies say he's the one who gets Junior into trouble.

My sleep that night was restless, and for the first time, I actually dreamed about the robbery. Just as I was about to snatch the mask from one of the robbers, I woke up. It was dark and I glanced at my clock. Two thirty. Groaning, I turned over and went back to sleep. Tomorrow I'd talk to Phoebe. If I could find her.

I awakened to a rolling grumble of thunder. Flipping over onto my side, I groaned. Another rainy day. I yawned and opened my eyes then sat up so fast I knocked a glass of water off my bedside table. Surely that wasn't snow? When it was thundering?

I rushed to the window, shivering in my bare feet. Great cotton-ball puffs floated from the sky, and at least three or four inches of snow covered the ground. Excitement tickled my stomach as I rushed around the room, donning sweatpants and shirt, thick angora socks, and the snow boots I hadn't had an opportunity to use yet. I'd thought the old folks were pulling my leg when they'd told me about thunder snow, but here it was. If the information I'd received was true, thunder snow could result in a foot or more in a few hours.

I grabbed my new down jacket from the coat closet and slipped it on as I headed out the front door.

Across the street, the three Hansen children had a snow fort almost finished. They must have gotten up at the crack of dawn. I waved to them and before I knew it, snowballs pelted me from head to toe. I put my hands over my face and, from between my fingers, saw their well-stocked arsenal.

"Okay, you guys. No fair. Give me time to get my ammo ready." I was answered with whoops of laughter and a new barrage of frozen missiles.

Swooping down, I scooped up a handful of snow and packed it into a ball. By the time I'd thrown it, missing my mark, my face was icy with slush. Laughing, I surrendered and made a beeline back to the house.

The bay window framed five laughing faces, and as I crashed through the door, the seniors rushed into the foyer, chortling with glee. Even Martin guffawed.

"I haven't seen such a one-sided snowball fight in a long time," Miss Jane said with a giggle.

"Hhmph," Frank retorted. "I haven't, either. You need some lessons, Victoria." He patted my shoulder as he passed by on his way to the dining room.

A strange combination of joy and sadness struck me. *Lord, please don't let it be Frank.*

"You'd better get out of those wet clothes and boots, dear," Miss Georgina said, still smiling.

"You're right." I yanked off the boots and dropped them on the throw rug by the door then kissed her softly on the cheek before heading up the stairs.

Breakfast waited on the buffet when I got back downstairs. I filled a plate with bacon, scrambled eggs, and toast then joined the seniors at the table. Miss Evalina smiled, glancing around at her friends. "Do you remember the Howards' big old sleigh?"

"Oh, yes!" Miss Jane clapped her hands. "Sally was so proud of that sleigh. It easily sat ten people. The only one in the county that carried so many."

Miss Georgina chimed in. "Remember the times we lined up four or five sleighs in a row and went to Bright Springs or Hannahsville for a play party? The sleigh bells could be heard from miles away."

I was enjoying their reminiscing so much, I didn't want to interrupt, so I made a mental note to ask Miss Georgina later what a play party was.

Martin laughed out loud. "Yeah, and remember how Frank used to finagle around to make sure he could sit with Ev . . ." He stopped and gave an embarrassed cough. "Sorry."

Cringing, I glanced at Miss Evalina. A sweet blush spread across her face, accompanied by a tinge of amusement. I shifted my gaze to Frank and saw a grin form at the side of his mouth. He turned his head, and I caught him flash a slight wink toward Miss Evalina, who ducked her head, suddenly very interested in spreading blackberry jam on her toast.

Okay, what's going on here? Glancing around the table, I saw from the cocked eyebrows and slight frowns displayed on the others' faces, they were as much in the dark as I was. A burst of wisdom convinced me to mind my own business for a change.

After breakfast, the ladies helped me clear the table away, a small chore they insisted on performing every morning. When the table was cleared and the dishes deposited on a counter in the kitchen, they went down to the recreation room and I headed upstairs to change bed linens and do some dusting. There was really no dusting to do in Frank's or the ladies' rooms. Martin, however, didn't seem to care if dust collected or not, so I spent a little longer in his room. I sighed at the stack of comics next to his chair. I'd learned long ago not to bother that stack, and I could just imagine the dust underneath.

Suddenly, I caught my breath sharply and stopped in my tracks. Why was Martin so particular about those old comics? A thread of suspicion weaved its way into my mind. Could he have something hidden in that pile? After all, if he'd robbed a bank when he was young, who was to know for sure that a crooked streak wasn't still residing in him? I hesitated. I had absolutely no evidence that Martin was involved in the robbery or Miss Aggie's disappearance. *But what if he was?*

I walked to the door and peeked out into the hallway then closed the door softly. I sat on the floor next to the stack and started with the top comic. I searched through each one till I reached the bottom, finding nothing at all. I replaced the comics in the correct order and stood. Of course, he could still be involved, even if I hadn't found anything incriminating in the comics. I bit my lip and pushed down the thought. Had I suddenly developed a suspicious nature? No, I had to admit I'd had the tendency most of my life. The only two people I'd ever completely trusted were Grandpa and Grandma. They were the only ones I always knew I could count on.

What about Me, Victoria? Do you trust Me? I felt a knot form in my throat and gulped it down. Did I trust God? I always said I did, thought I did. I remembered Benjamin's words the previous night. *Have you thought of trusting God?* Did I trust Him, without reservation? Sudden tears rushed to my eyes. *I want to trust You that way, Lord. But it's so hard.*

Sighing, I got up and changed the linens on Martin's bed then took them down to the basement and started the washer. Restlessness nibbled at my thoughts as I hiked back up the stairs. Corky glanced up from the table where he sat making out his weekly grocery list. Suddenly I thought of my plan concerning Phoebe. She and Corky had either gotten chummy mighty fast or they'd known each other all along. How could I convince her to open up to me? Or at least let something slip.

"Corky, will you see Phoebe in the next few days?" I asked.

He jerked his head up and stared at me then smiled. "Maybe."

“I’d thought of inviting her to lunch one day.”

A closed look replaced the smile. “Why would you do that?”

Surprise caused me to speak sharper than I intended. “I didn’t know I needed to give you a reason when I want to invite someone to lunch, Corky.”

His face relaxed. “Sorry. I didn’t mean it to sound that way. It’s just that she might leave town for a while.”

“Really? Where’s she going?”

“Abilene, Texas. Her sister is having a baby, and she might help out for a couple of weeks.” He went back to his list.

Hmmm, maybe I’d better get myself over to the bank before she goes. And on second thought, maybe lunch away from the house would be better. I went to the foyer door and peered out one of the tall, narrow windows at the side. The thunder had stopped but snow still fell. I had no idea how deep the drifts were in the street, but I could walk to the bank in fifteen minutes. Twenty minutes later I stepped into the bank and stomped snow off my boots.

The lobby was empty, and the first person I saw was Phoebe staring at me from behind her teller window. I grinned and marched over. “Hi, Phoebe.”

“Hello, Victoria,” she said in a near whisper. Was I that scary? Or had someone warned her not to talk to me? "How can I help you?"

"I need to withdraw a little cash." I picked up a withdrawal slip and filled in the information then slipped it through the window to her.

Phoebe got the cash from the drawer and counted it back to me in silence.

"Thank you. I wondered if you'd like to have lunch one day this week? As much as I love the seniors, sometimes I really crave spending some time with someone closer to my own age."

"Oh, well . . ."

"I thought we could go to Manuelo's if you like Mexican food. Or any place you'd like."

"Well," she said, "I'd love to, but I'm going to Texas soon, and I'm not sure when I'm leaving."

"Yes, Corky told me." Let her think he was agreeable to the idea. "So, I thought tomorrow, if you're free?"

"Corky knows?" she asked breathlessly.

"Umm-hmm." Okay, I did mention inviting her to lunch.

The drapes were closed across the bay window, and a log fire crackled and popped in the little corner fireplace. How cozy everything appeared. If only it were so. Benjamin had dropped by late in the afternoon, and I'd asked him to stay. I'd decided after Corky left would be a good time to lay everything out for scrutiny, including the suspicions crowding my mind. Maybe if we put our heads together we could come up with some ideas.

Everyone looked at me expectantly, so I set my cup down and picked up the notebook I'd brought with me.

"As we all know, it's been three weeks since Miss Aggie disappeared." I paused as a choked sob escaped Miss Georgina's throat.

She dabbed her eyes and gave me an apologetic glance. "I'm sorry."

"It's all right. I feel like crying, too."

"It seems we're nowhere nearer the truth than when we started," Martin snapped. "If that sheriff knows anything, he's keeping quiet about it." Somber nods greeted his comment. Benjamin shifted in his chair and looked at me questioningly.

"Okay," I continued. "After the robbery and Miss Aggie's disappearance, I started jotting down some possible suspects. I think it's time to share everything with you." I cleared my throat. "Some of you aren't going to like a few of my thoughts. In fact, a few of you are on the list."

"What?" Martin glared, his eyebrows raised a notch.

"Do you suspect me, Victoria?" Miss Georgina asked in a tiny voice. I hastened to soothe her.

"Shhh. Please. Let me explain." I glanced around the room. Miss Jane and Miss Georgina had never once come under suspicion as far as I was concerned. My attention turned to Miss Evalina. How could I have ever suspected her? I hesitated to even mention it for fear of humiliating her. But in all fairness, I had to put it all on the table for scrutiny in case the truth should dawn on someone. Martin. Frank. I could only pray neither of them was guilty of whatever had happened to Miss Aggie.

I opened my notebook. "All right. The robbery took place about the time Miss Aggie left for the library. As far as we know, no one in town has seen her since." Nods assured me I had their attention.

"In the beginning, we automatically assumed Miss Aggie had been abducted by the robbers. Next, we found out about Miss Aggie's computer activity and thought perhaps she'd met someone online who had harmed her in some way." I shuddered. It could so easily have happened that way. "When the computer files turned out to be innocent, that fear was put to rest. By the way, I checked my computer, too, and there was no sign Miss Aggie had used it at all."

"Oh, my," Miss Jane sputtered. "Your computer never crossed my mind."

I glanced at my list and hesitated then took the plunge. "Benjamin and I saw Frank coming out of a pawn shop in Middle Point, and since Frank refused to tell us why he was there, well, there's the possibility he was selling Miss Aggie's missing diamonds."

"What?" The word exploded from Frank's mouth, and his face reddened.

"Please let me continue, Frank. You can say what you like when I'm finished." Deep furrows appeared between his eyes, and he glowered but didn't say anything else. The disapproving look Miss Evalina shot my way said enough.

I jumped as a log fell, scattering sparks and embers. Everyone was glaring at me except Benjamin. I groaned inwardly. If they were mad at me now, what would their reaction be to my next statement?

"Okay, now please don't anyone scream at me. But for just a teeny little while I considered the possibility that maybe, but probably not, Miss Evalina held a grudge against Miss Aggie because of Frank and . . ." My words trailed off, and I rushed the next words before the angry boarders had a chance to attack me. "But I'm convinced now she's totally innocent, and I never really thought she wasn't."

"Victoria Storm, you've gone too far," Frank thundered, standing and shaking his finger at me. "If you want to accuse me, go ahead, but to think this angel could ever . . ."

"Shame on you, Victoria," Miss Georgina said and frowned pointedly in my direction.

Miss Evalina stood. "Everyone calm down. Victoria is trying to find out what happened to Aggie and has to investigate even the smallest possibilities. And besides, she apologized to me. Frank, sit down. Let her finish." She sat and pulled him down beside her.

I heard a smothered laugh and glanced to see Benjamin attempting to hide a grin behind his hand. Tossing him an indignant scowl, I got up and declared that I was leaving the room until everyone collected themselves.

"Don't be ridiculous, Victoria. Sit down and finish your report." Miss Evalina frowned.

Report? Did she think I was one of her students? I flopped back into my chair. I rubbed a hand across my forehead then took a quick look at the notebook. "As you all know, I drove to Jefferson City a few days ago to talk to Simon Pennington." With relief, I noticed they'd calmed down and were listening again. "I told you most of what happened that day, but not everything. I saw a family portrait when I was there, and Simon's son bore a striking resemblance to Corky."

"Corky? Our Corky?" Miss Jane asked, sitting forward in her chair.

"Yes, Miss Jane. That night, Miss Evalina and I went through the albums in Miss Aggie's room and found pictures of Simon's son, Dane, as a boy. We also found the same one I'd seen at the Penningtons' home."

"So Corky is Miss Aggie's brother's grandson? Aggie's great-nephew? Or would that be great-great-nephew?" Miss Georgina seemed confused, and I couldn't blame her. I was confused myself.

"Now, Georgina, Victoria didn't say Corky is Dane Pennington. Only that the photo of the young boy bears a resemblance to him. We don't know for sure."

"That's right. I hate to think Corky had anything to do with Miss Aggie's disappearance, but in addition to the picture, the fact is he's acted strangely lately." I told them about finding him upstairs and about him listening at the door when we discussed Miss Aggie.

"Oh, so now it's Corky you suspect instead of me," Frank piped up with a glint in his eyes.

"As a matter of fact, Mr. Cordell, you've been awfully chummy with Corky lately," I said.

He looked at me strangely then shook his head. "Okay, I guess it's time I told you what's been going on. Especially in light of this Dane Pennington thing."

I inhaled sharply. Was Frank going to confess? Was this it? I saw Benjamin shift in his chair and turn on a small recorder.

"I ran into Corky one day as he came out of a pawn shop in Branson. He said he was looking for a subwoofer, whatever that is. But I couldn't help thinking about the diamonds." He looked me in the eye. "I started tailing him after that. The day you saw me in Middle Point, I'd left the shop right after Corky. You just missed him. I tried to get some information from the guy in the shop, but he wouldn't tell me anything. After that, I continued following him every chance I got. He's gone to just about all the pawn shops around here."

Excitement boiled up inside me. I didn't doubt Frank for a moment. And this was another indication Corky might be involved in Miss Aggie's disappearance. We needed to get this information to the sheriff. Even without proof, it was too important to keep from him. But would he just laugh in our faces again?

16

The fire had burned down to embers, and still Benjamin and I hadn't said good night. The seniors had gone to bed a couple of hours ago, and he and I had tossed around the idea of taking our information to Sheriff Turner. Benjamin thought we should go to him right away, but I was hesitant.

"Ben, I'd really rather wait awhile until we can gather more evidence."

He reached over and tucked in a strand of hair that had come loose from my hastily arranged ponytail. "I know how he's treated your ideas so far. But I don't want to see you get yourself into trouble for withholding evidence. That's serious, Vickie."

He had a point. But I wasn't sure it was evidence and didn't want Corky to find out until I was sure. However, I didn't want Benjamin taking matters into his own hands either.

I yawned. "Okay, you're probably right. Maybe I'll tell him in the morning."

He ran his thumb down my cheek and then cupped my chin in his hand. "I think I'd better go so you can get some sleep."

"Yeah," I said, yawning again. "I wanted to ask you something, though."

"Okay." He removed his hand and smiled.

"Ben, you had a lot of faith when you were a boy. I can't believe you've stopped believing." I tensed as I waited for his answer.

He leaned back on the sofa cushion, facing me. "Vickie, I don't think I want to talk about it."

"What changed your mind about God? What made you stop believing in the first place?"

An expression of pain crossed his face, and I wondered if I should have asked the question.

"I think after Mom left and Dad fell to pieces, my faith started to crumble. But Frank and Betty were so good to me and had such a strong relationship with God, it kept me from totally falling away." He swiped a hand across his eyes as though wiping away memories.

"When I started covering homicide for the paper in Kansas City, I saw and heard things that made me question how a loving God could let such horrors occur. Especially when the victims were children. I had trouble reconciling those atrocities to the belief in a loving God. My faith got rattled, Vickie. After our talk the night Miss Aggie disappeared, I started thinking about how much I used to believe and about the things you'd said. I dug out the family Bible my grandfather used to preach from. Some of the pages are missing, but I started reading it anyway. I've been searching and searching. But I can't find my faith again. I've tried." I scooted closer to him and took his hand. He turned it over and gave mine a squeeze.

"But, Benjamin, God isn't responsible for the evil in the world. That comes when people choose to turn their backs on Him. He cries over the children, too. And over all the horrors you've seen. But He's given us free will to choose how we live. Some choose to walk in darkness."

He squeezed my hand again.

"Thank you for caring so much, sweetheart." His voice was husky with emotion. "I wish I could truly believe again. Believe God really cares."

I looked into his eyes, and my heart lurched at the pain there.

"You have to choose to believe, Ben. Ask Him. He'll help you."

No words could cover what I was feeling at that moment. The thought of what Benjamin had gone through tightened my chest with grief, but at the same time, I knew he had to get past it and trust God no matter what.

Finally I choked out, "I'll be praying for you, Ben." He reached out two fingers and wiped tears from my face. "Thanks, honey. And I think maybe I'll do some praying myself."

"Then you'll find your faith again. I know you will."

We stood, and he gave me a quick hug. "Tomorrow, I'll head to Kansas City to do some checking on Dane Pennington. Promise you won't confront Corky until I get back. Okay?"

"I promise. Be careful driving, though. The roads may be bad."

“They’ll be fine once I get to Springfield. Besides, I’m used to driving on icy and snow-packed roads, remember? I’ve lived through a lot of Missouri winters.”

I stood in the darkness and watched him leave, his words running through my mind. *Lord, draw Benjamin to You. I know faith is still there. Show me how to help him. But if he makes the wrong choice, help me to guard my heart.*

I sighed, went in to check all the door locks, then went down to see about Buster. He whined and wagged his tail, eager to see me.

“Come on, boy,” I said, making a sudden decision. “You’re sleeping in my room tonight.” Although I was sure he’d just wag his tail if Corky appeared beside my bed with a meat cleaver in the middle of the night.

He followed me up the stairs to the kitchen where I double-checked the deadbolt on the door to the garage. I grabbed a fresh bottle of water from the refrigerator and went up to my room. Buster seemed a little bit puzzled and stood in the hallway until I called him in. When he was sure I meant it, he bounded into the room and up to the middle of my bed.

“Unh-unh, Buster boy. You get the chair.”

In the middle of the night I woke up. Buster lay in front of the door, his eyes half open. Turning over, I drifted off to sleep with a delicious feeling of safety. When Buster and I came down the next morning, five pairs of eyes gawked at us from the foyer.

"What? You've never seen a dog before?"

"I've never seen one upstairs in this house before," Martin muttered. "Next thing I know, he'll be in my room. He'd better not mess with my comics."

I laughed and took Buster to the basement then walked him around to the backyard where I left him playing in three-foot snowdrifts.

When I went inside, I realized there was no sign of breakfast anywhere. Miss Jane was poking around in the refrigerator.

"Where's Corky?"

"He called and said his truck wouldn't start and he was getting a jump from someone."

"Here, let me take those eggs. I'll cook." I took the carton she handed me and removed a bowl from the cupboard.

"I'll help," she said, taking bacon from the refrigerator. "You scramble and I'll fry some bacon." She took two fry pans from the black metal pot rack. I was happy to let her help. Miss Jane was a wonderful cook.

After a more than adequate breakfast, I decided I'd put off paperwork too long, so I headed for my office. The snow had finally stopped sometime during the night, but the deep drifts and bitter cold winds made it doubtful that Phoebe and I could keep our lunch date. By the time I shut my computer down, it was almost lunchtime, with still no sign of Corky.

I drifted through the downstairs rooms, making small talk with the seniors. As I walked past the rarely used back parlor, I heard a murmur of voices through the closed door. Curious, I opened the door a crack.

Frank and Miss Evalina sat holding hands on the loveseat next to the tiny, curtain-frilled window. Frank was looking down at Miss Evalina with tenderness. "Eva, can you forgive me for being such a fool?"

She reached her frail hand up and touched his face. "I forgave you long ago. You know that."

"If only I'd come back to Cedar Chapel after I'd come to my senses," he said with a shake of his head. "But I thought you must hate me. I didn't think there would be any use."

"It's all right, Frank. I know you loved Betty. And that's all right, too."

Softly, I closed the door and tiptoed away. I'd already heard more than I had any business hearing. I turned when I heard the foyer door open, and Corky and Phoebe crashed through, their laughter reverberating down the hallway.

"Oh. Victoria. Hello," Phoebe said breathlessly. Her face was pink, and I wasn't sure if it was from the cold or if she was blushing.

"Phoebe, what a surprise. Have the road crews been out, Corky?" I determined to keep the conversation as normal as possible.

"Yes," he answered as he helped Phoebe remove her coat. "They cleared the major streets this morning. We followed the snow plow around this neighborhood right up to your door." He grinned. "I figured since you and Phoebe were supposed to have lunch, maybe you'd rather have it here because of the drifts."

As I examined his relaxed face, I wondered how a kidnapper-bank-robber-murderer could look so cheerful and innocent. But he looked a little smug, too. Had he been afraid for Phoebe and me to have lunch alone? Probably.

"Is something wrong? I'm sorry I couldn't get here sooner."

"It's okay, but I'm afraid lunch will be leftover chili." I turned to the girl, who stood looking a little uncertain. "Phoebe, I'm so glad you came. Hope you like chili."

"Chili sounds wonderful," Phoebe exclaimed, her eyes bright as she smiled at Corky.

Okay, so she didn't act like a vicious conspirator, and neither did he. But I wasn't about to let them charm me from my pursuit of the truth.

Lunch was fun. A lot of fun. Corky had us practically in tears from laughing so hard through the meal. I couldn't help it. It was difficult to stay objective. Afterward, as we sat around the fire in the parlor, I questioned

Phoebe about the robbers again, but she said she hadn't observed anything familiar about them. Either she was telling the truth or she should have been on Broadway. Corky prepared a light meal that could be warmed up and served at dinnertime; then he left to escort Phoebe back to the bank. I'd told him he could have the rest of the afternoon off. No sense in his driving on the streets more than he had to.

Late that afternoon Benjamin called. So far, he hadn't found out much about Dane Pennington, but he refused to give up. He had connections with several news sources in the city and planned to make the rounds the next day.

"Benjamin, I'm not sure he's Corky."

"What do you mean? Has something happened?"

"No, not really. I'm just not sure anymore."

He snorted. "Well, we've never been sure. That's why I'm here, remember?"

"I know, but . . . I'm just so confused."

"I know you are, honey."

Neither of us spoke for a moment.

"Victoria?"

"Yes?"

He cleared his throat. "Nothing. I just wanted to say your name. See you when I get back."

I hung up the phone and leaned against the wall. Why had I ever thought I could solve this mystery? I was no closer to finding Miss Aggie than I'd been the day she disappeared.

"Why are you leaning against the wall like that, Victoria? Don't you know oils from the body and hair are bad for wallpaper?"

I shoved away from the wall and smiled at Miss Georgina. She worried over the silliest things sometimes.

"You're right. I'll try to remember not to do that. Wanna help me get supper warmed up?"

She giggled and gave me a forgiving pat on the shoulder. "Just the two of us? Jane's not going to take over?"

"No," I said, laughing. "We won't let Miss Jane in the kitchen this time."

She giggled again, and we walked into the kitchen arm in arm. By the time we had everything laid out on the buffet, the rest of the boarders had made their way to the dining room.

Miss Evalina was unusually quiet during dinner. Afterward, she helped clear the table and went up to her room. The rest gathered around the piano in the parlor while Miss Georgina played songs from the thirties and forties, some of them rather lively tunes.

When everyone retired for the night, I straightened up the parlor, peeked in on Buster, and went upstairs. Light shone from Miss Evalina's room, and I stood outside her door for a moment wondering if I should intrude. Finally, I knocked lightly.

"Come in," she called softly.

I entered the room to find her sitting fully dressed in the rocker, bent over an old photo album.

She looked up, and a smile curved her lips. A smile that didn't reach her eyes.

"I was just going through these old photos of Frank and me. Look, Victoria. We were only nine years old here."

I bent over her shoulder and perused the faded black-and-white photo. Two children perched on the back of a two-toned Shetland pony. The girl sat with her legs hanging ladylike off to one side, an enormous bow in her hair and a dainty smile on her face. Behind her, the boy sat astride the horse, his elbow propped on the girl's shoulder and his tongue sticking out at whoever stood behind the camera.

I chuckled. "Looks like someone was having fun."

"Frank and I always had fun together." She sighed and closed the album. "He asked me to marry him today."

I inhaled sharply. I suppose I should have expected it, but honestly, a marriage proposal had never crossed my mind.

"I told him I'd think about it." She peered at me through her aged blue eyes. "I suppose you think I'm addled to even consider such a thing."

"Not at all, Miss Evalina. You've loved Frank for a long time. There wouldn't be anything wrong with your marrying him, if that's what you want to do."

"And there lies the question. Do I want to?" She rubbed her temples.

"Well, only you can decide that. Maybe you should pray about it for a while."

Her smile was pensive. "I've prayed about it for years. I always knew he'd ask one day, but I still don't know the answer."

"I'd say do what you think is best for you and Frank."

She gave me a strange look, and then her eyes crinkled with amusement. "You've hit the nail on the head, as they say, my dear."

She stood and stretched. "Now I think I'll get some sleep. I'll see you in the morning."

At breakfast the next morning, Miss Evalina's answer seemed obvious. She and Frank flirted like a couple of schoolchildren. It seemed the air had cleared for everyone and the tension was gone. I could hardly wait for the announcement, but as it turned out, I'd have to. The roads were clear enough that all the boarders decided to go to the center.

"Don't expect us for lunch, this is bingo day," Martin said as he got into Frank's car. I was a little bit surprised to see Miss Evalina climb into Miss Jane's Caddy.

I tried to call Benjamin, but he didn't answer his cell phone. Corky needed a few things from the supermarket, so I got into my winter garb and asked for his list. I was getting antsy hanging around the house. As I pulled out of the garage, I noticed the children across the street pummeling each other from behind the fort and a snow-covered corner shrub.

With a grin, I stopped the car, reached out the door, and grabbed a handful of snow. Packing it as tightly as I could, I crept out of the car, stood up quickly, and threw the icy missile as hard as I could. A yell of protest gave proof it had landed on someone. I slipped in quickly behind the wheel, a giggle starting deep in my stomach and rippling from my throat. I peeled out of the driveway and down the street, with a deluge of snowballs pelting after me. When I pulled back into the garage an hour later, I looked carefully before leaving the car and hurrying into the kitchen.

"Hey, what did you do to the kids across the street?" Corky asked as I breezed in.

"Why?" I asked innocently, hoping their parents weren't angry.

"They left you this note." He tossed it to me with a grin.

In big block letters I read:

BEWARE THE STORM FORCE! WE'LL BE WAITING!

Laughing, I recounted my unfair attack. I wasn't too sure I wanted to venture out anytime soon, though.

"Oh, you have a message from Benjamin, too.

He said to tell you he's staying over another day. He'll try to call later."

I glanced at Corky, wondering if he knew where Benjamin was. Well, there were a lot of reasons to go to Kansas City. After all, Benjamin owned a newspaper.

I looked out the window, eager for the seniors to get back. I wondered when and how Frank and Miss Evalina would make their announcement. Maybe they'd gather us into the parlor after dinner to tell their news. I've always been a romantic, and happy endings turn me to mush.

I waited through dinner, canasta, and good nights with still no announcement. Finally, I couldn't stand it any longer and tapped on Miss Evalina's door.

"It's perfectly simple, dear," she explained. "I told him no."

I stood gaping. "But why? You love each other."

"Of course we do. But we loved each other back then, too. How could I be sure another pretty face wouldn't come along and turn his head again?" I walked to my room, stunned, and a little bit disappointed. Then as I shut the door behind me, I chuckled. Because I had a feeling Miss Evalina was simply getting a smidgen of revenge at last. Hopefully, Frank wouldn't give up. But I was pretty sure it would take more than candy from Betty's to win Miss Evalina's hand in marriage.

17

The phone's shrill ring jolted me awake. In the darkness, I slammed my hand over, knocking the phone off its cradle and onto the floor. Hanging off the side of the bed, I managed to retrieve it then scramble upright.

"Hello," I sputtered into the phone.

"What's wrong?" Benjamin sounded worried.

"Nothing. The phone startled me." I glanced at the clock on the bedside table. "For crying out loud, it's only five thirty."

"I know. Sorry. I've been up all night and thought I'd try to catch a couple hours sleep. I'm having some problems with my truck and may not be back until tomorrow. But I wanted you to know right away that Corky is, without a doubt, Dane Pennington."

I gasped, suddenly wide awake.

"I found out where Pennington attended Culinary Arts School and talked to some people there. Seems he was quite the honor student. There were photos of him. It's Corky all right."

"Oh, no—I'd hoped—"

"I know. But listen, Vic. The picture painted by his instructors just doesn't line up with that of a criminal. Maybe he's not involved after all."

"Then why did he keep his identity a secret? That doesn't make sense."

"I know it looks that way. All I'm saying is there's a possibility he's at Cedar Lodge for a totally innocent reason."

I huffed. "Okay, Benjamin. It's obvious you don't want me to go to the sheriff. So why are you telling me at all?"

"Because I'm still not sure about it. I'd like for you to be careful. You and the seniors should stay together, just in case. But try not to let him know you're aware of his identity."

I sighed and swung my legs off the bed, slipping my feet into fuzzy pink slippers. "When do you think you'll be back, Benjamin?"

"If they don't have my car ready by evening, I'll fly to Springfield and rent a car there. Don't worry. I'll be home tomorrow afternoon, one way or the other." I could hear his steady breathing through the phone. "Promise me you'll be careful and not do anything foolish."

"Foolish?" My voice rose in sync with my disappointment.

"Okay, okay, I shouldn't have said foolish. Calm down. Just don't get hurt, honey. Please."

"I won't," I said, calming at his words. "I promise you that."

We said good-bye, and I grabbed fresh clothing then jumped into the shower. Maybe Mr. Dane Pennington had his instructors fooled, but I wasn't falling for his charade.

At six thirty I walked into the dining room. The

seniors were lined up, plates in hand, as Corky dished eggs into a chafing dish on the buffet. He hummed as he worked then flashed me a grin as he turned and saw me in the doorway.

"Good morning, Victoria. I hope you're hungry. I went on a cooking spree this morning." He motioned to the heaping baskets of muffins, a chafing dish of scrambled eggs, bacon, link sausage, a bowl of fresh fruit, and another chafing dish of steaming oatmeal.

I gave him an abrupt nod. "Thank you, Corky. Everything looks and smells delicious." I filled a plate and sat at the head of the dining table. I still felt conspicuous there. Like a child stealing her father's chair. Only in this case, the chair belonged to Grandpa and then Grandma.

My mind revolved around Benjamin's information about Corky. And his insistence that Corky was, in all likelihood, innocent of Miss Aggie's disappearance. But . . . I hadn't actually promised him I wouldn't go talk to the sheriff, and I had every intention of doing just that. Even though every other attempt to share information with the sheriff had flopped, surely he'd agree there was no reason for Dane Pennington to hide his identity unless he was up to no good.

Pulling myself from my thoughts, I asked the seniors if they'd like to go for a drive.

Martin snorted. "Drive? Why would anyone want to take a drive in this mess? There's dirty piles of snow everywhere."

Nods of agreement met his statement, but finally, with the use of eye and facial expressions, I got it across to them that something was up. After breakfast, they piled grudgingly into the van, amid murmuring, head shaking, and disgusted looks thrown my way.

I backed out of the drive. “Okay, I’ll explain in a minute.”

On the way to the courthouse, I told them what Benjamin’s investigation had turned up and informed them I was taking the information to the sheriff.

“But didn’t you just say Benjamin thinks Corky is innocent?” Miss Jane asked.

“Well, yes. But I’m not convinced.”

“I agree,” Miss Evalina said. “Why would an innocent man hide his identity?”

“Ah . . . I dunno,” Frank said. “Benjamin wouldn’t think Corky was innocent without a good reason.”

“Maybe,” Martin said. “Maybe not. Could be he’s involved, too.”

“What do you mean by that?” Frank yelled.

Guffaws exploded from Martin. “I knew I could get you riled if I said something derogatory about your boy.”

“Why, you old . . .”

Miss Evalina twisted in her seat and glared at both men. “You two stop it right now. You’re behaving like children.”

I tossed her a look of gratitude as I slid the van

into a parking spot in front of the courthouse. We filed through the door and were met by a frowning Tom, who stood and came from behind his cubby.

"Look," he said with a belligerent glare. "Sheriff Turner doesn't want to see you nutcases. So why don't you turn around and get on out of here."

"Excuse me?" Miss Evalina pushed forward, followed closely by the rest of the gang. "Would you like to be sued for defamation of character, young man?"

"Huh?" Tom backed up nervously and scooted behind the window.

"That's what I thought. Don't bother to show us in. We know the direction to Bob's office." With that, she led the way as we tromped after her, grins tugging at our lips.

Sheriff Turner jumped up as we filed into his office. The FBI agent sat in a chair to the left of his desk.

"What clues have you turned up now, Victoria?" the sheriff asked sarcastically.

Miss Evalina moved aside, and I planted my feet on the floor in front of the desk. "It just so happens, Sheriff, we have some very important information for you."

"Ah, of course you do," he said with a side grin to the agent. "Okay, you tell me this information, and I'll decide how important it is."

"Laugh at this, Sheriff," I said. "I've received information that Corky Daniels is actually none other than Dane Pennington, a great-nephew or something of Miss Aggie's."

With a great sense of satisfaction, I watched the sheriff's face go from amiable to dead serious. He glanced quickly at the agent, who shook his head ever so slightly.

Sheriff Turner's face was unreadable as he smiled at me. "Well, thank you for the information. I'll check it out. Now if you'll excuse me, I've got law enforcing to do."

Miss Evalina gasped and leaned over the sheriff's desk till she stood almost nose to nose with him. "Bob Turner, what in the world is wrong with you? Victoria has proof positive that Dane Pennington came to town and took employment at Cedar Lodge with a false identity in order to keep his own a secret. If you don't think that's suspicious, you're a very foolish man."

The sheriff's face flamed. "Now, Miss Evalina. I said I'd check it out and I will. But I can't just drop everything to investigate every charge that's brought to my attention. And I haven't seen any proof of motive yet."

"Hhmph!" She gave him one last glare and turned. "Let's get out of here. I can assure you all Bob Turner won't get my vote at the next election."

We walked out and climbed into the van. "Now what?" I asked. "If the sheriff won't help us, what can we do?"

"I guess we could search Corky's apartment."

We all stared at Martin in incredulous silence.

He gave an embarrassed cough and tugged at his lip.

"Martin, that's breaking and entering. We can't do that." I couldn't help but wish we could, though.

"Maybe Martin has an idea there," Frank said, scratching his head. "We might find something the sheriff would have to take seriously."

Miss Georgina whimpered. "Like Victoria said, that's breaking and entering. We could all go to jail."

"Oh, stop whining," Miss Jane huffed. "Who says we have to get caught? And even if we do, Bob's not going to throw us in jail. The most he'd do is fine us or something."

I would have loved to think Miss Jane was right, but I had a hunch Sheriff Turner would be all too happy to throw us all in jail.

"I don't think we'd better do that," I said.

"I think we should," Frank argued. "Martin, you and I can take care of it if the ladies want to go back to the lodge."

"Well, I'm not going back to the lodge," Miss Jane sputtered. "I'm going to do anything I can to help find Aggie."

"While I understand Victoria's concern, and I've never been anything but a law-abiding citizen, this is different. I'm coming along, too." Miss Evalina's voice and countenance were determined, and I knew I'd lost this battle.

"All right, if you have your minds set to do this, I'll go with you, but we need to wait until dark."

"How can we do that?" Martin asked with a scornful glance my way. "Corky lives there, you know."

"Yes, but I happen to know he has a date with Phoebe tonight. So, how do you propose we get into the apartment?"

"Well," he said hesitantly, "I sort of know how to pick locks."

Miss Jane's black Cadillac rolled slowly through the dark streets of Cedar Chapel. At ten o'clock, there was very little traffic on the street, and Miss Jane was sticking to back streets as much as possible. The only sound was the sloshing of melting snow under the heavy tires.

I sat between Frank and Martin in the wide backseat with my camera on my lap, while Miss Georgina sat in the front, wedged between Miss Jane and Miss Evalina. She'd insisted right up to the last minute she had no intention of taking part in a crime, but at the end she couldn't face being left alone at the lodge.

Miss Jane turned onto the highway and headed toward Corky's apartment fourplex on the outskirts of town. She pulled into the gravel driveway and around to the back of the units. During any other season, the apartments would all be occupied, but this time of year, few tourists remained in Cedar Chapel. Only one unit besides Corky's was rented. A dim light shone in the window at the far end of the building.

"His job application says apartment A," I offered.

"I'll look," Martin said. "The rest of you stay here till I get back." He got no argument there. We could barely see his shadow as he slunk toward the building.

After what seemed an eternity, the back door of the car swung open. Georgina screeched.

"Shhh." Miss Jane touched her fingers to the nervous woman's lips.

"Dang it, Georgina, pipe down," Martin snapped.

"Sorry," she squeaked. "I didn't know it was you."

"Come on. I've got the door unlocked."

Lord, please forgive us for this. I must have spoken aloud because I heard several whispered "amens." We climbed out and tiptoed over to the door. When we went in, Frank and Martin made sure all the blinds were drawn and the drapes pulled shut before they turned on a couple of lamps. I glanced around at Corky's combined living and dining area. The room was neat and clean. Well, as neat and clean as you'd expect a bachelor's apartment to be. Magazines were scattered all over the tables and spilled over onto the floor. I bent over the coffee table and took a peek at the covers of a couple. They were both culinary magazines. Checking out the rest, I found them to be mostly the same with a few selections of old homes. I stood up. Miss Jane and Miss Georgina were removing books from a bookcase one by one and shaking the books. Good idea. Miss Evalina stood before a painting on the wall, running her fingers around the edge of the frame. I could hear the men moving around in the bedroom and bath.

"Ha!" Frank's exclamation could be heard all over the apartment, and we all rushed into the bedroom to see him standing over a corner desk. One of the drawers stood open, and Frank held up some photographs. With a grin and a flourish, he spread them out on the desktop. "Here's your evidence, Victoria."

The photos were mostly old, some very old. I held up one, of an old mansion standing in a heavily wooded area. The lawn in front was lush and green. There were several pictures of the same house from different angles. In one of them a family stood in front of the wide pillared porch. I held it up for Miss Evalina. Her eyes glistened as she reached for the picture.

"This is Aggie and her family. She was seven or eight here, and this must have been one of the few summers Forrest spent at home." Miss Evalina's eyes almost devoured the picture. "This was probably taken at her birthday party. If so, we were around somewhere. Look, Jane, Georgina."

Frank huffed. "Okay, ladies, I hate to break up the trip down memory lane. But you're missing the point here. And there's another picture here that may interest you more." He held it up and all three of the ladies gasped.

"I believe this is what we've been searching for."

The diamond pieces lay side by side on a silver tray. Even in black and white, the stones seemed to wink at me.

Miss Evalina's voice sounded strangled. "Aggie's insurance agent took these pictures when she had them insured."

Sorrow hung over the room. There was no doubt now that Corky had known about the diamonds. Did this mean Miss Aggie had been killed? For the jewels? *Oh, please, Lord. Please, no.*

My hands shook as I snapped picture after picture, wishing all the while I'd invested in a digital camera. We'd have to wait for Benjamin to develop them. "Let's put everything back the way we found it and get out of here," I whispered. "I think we have what we came for."

The drive back to the lodge was somber, with an occasional sob from the front seat. Confusion roiled in my brain. I couldn't seem to think clearly.

When we arrived back home, we went as one into the parlor and sat. No one seemed to notice the dying embers or the cold creeping into the room. The cold that crept into our hearts was much worse.

"Should we wake Bob up?" Miss Jane asked.

"I don't know, Miss Jane. I don't know what to do."

"We need to call him," Miss Evalina said. "He's the sheriff, whether we like it or not."

I nodded and Frank went to the phone. I was grateful they didn't expect me to make the call. I felt totally numb.

"Hi, Bob. Frank Cordell here. Sorry to wake you up so late, but we've discovered some new information."

Loud ranting from the receiver echoed through the room.

"But, Bob . . ." Frank looked at us in disbelief and laid the phone back down. "He hung up. I don't believe this. Bob's acting downright stupid. There's something wrong here."

With sudden decision, I stood. "All right. I guess we continue to handle this ourselves. I'm going to lock the film in the safe. Hopefully, Benjamin will be home by morning." I glanced at each of them. "Please, whatever you do, don't confront Corky. There's safety in numbers. Remember that."

Miss Georgina spoke up. "Maybe we should bolt the door with the inside bolts. He couldn't get in then."

"No, we can't do that," Frank explained. "We don't want to tip him off. After all, we have no real proof he's done anything except hide his identity. Surprise is the best bet."

I sent a smile of gratitude his way. Gratitude that he understood the situation and gratitude for his forgiveness of my suspicions of him. He reached over and hugged me.

Thank You, God, for these friends.

I woke to the sound of dripping water. Pulling the covers up over my ears, I tried to go back to sleep, but even the thick down comforter only muffled the constant *drip, drip, drip.* Growling, I pushed the covers back and sat up, blinking at the sunlight beaming in through the window. The drip was louder, but at least I had it located. I stood and walked to the window.

A glob of snow broke loose from the roof and crashed to the ground, followed by more dripping. Apparently, there'd been an unseasonable warm-up during the night. What a mess. Maybe I should rethink my love for Missouri winters.

Sighing, I headed for the shower. I had more important things to worry about than melting snow.

When I got downstairs, the smell of bacon and toasted bread wafted from the dining room. I found the buffet spread and ready, but no one in sight except Corky, who stood by the table with a puzzled look on his face.

"Aren't the others down yet?" I asked in as normal a voice as I could manage.

He shrugged. "I've no idea. They're usually in here waiting before I bring anything in."

Nodding, I left the room and headed for the

parlor, where I found them all, seated and speaking in low tones.

"Hey, let's eat breakfast." I rubbed my stomach and received a few nervous titters.

"We thought we'd better wait until you came down, Victoria," Miss Jane said. "We weren't sure how you wanted to handle the situation."

"I told them we should go on in there and act normal, but these two"—Martin pointed to Miss Jane and Miss Georgina—"wouldn't go in, and you told us to stick together."

"But, I didn't mean . . ." I stopped and smiled. "All right, let's go in together and try to act as though nothing is out of the ordinary."

"Are you going to call Benjamin?" Miss Evalina asked.

"I tried but didn't get an answer. He may be driving in heavy traffic on his way back and couldn't answer." I didn't want them to see my concern about not getting through to Benjamin.

"Or he may have found out too much and someone nabbed him." Martin guffawed and slapped his leg.

I decided to ignore him, and it appeared the others had the same idea as we walked in to breakfast together.

The stilted dialogue at the breakfast table wouldn't have fooled anyone, and the seniors kept darting questioning glances in my direction. Finally I asked pointedly if anyone was going to church today. At first all the response I got was stares, but after a moment Miss Evalina said, "Yes, as a matter of fact, I think we should all go."

She was met with reluctant agreement, but Miss Jane informed me she'd be home right after the service, and the others all nodded their agreement.

I breathed a sigh of relief as two vehicles pulled out of the driveway and headed down the street. There was no way they could have managed to behave normally all morning.

A couple of hours later, I sat at my computer wading through neglected e-mail when Corky tapped on the open door and came in.

"Yes, Corky? Do you need something?"

"Well, yeah. I need to know what's going on and why all the old folks are treating me like Jack the Ripper." Exasperation was written all over his face as he ran his fingers through his tight curls.

I looked at him as he stood there with his hair mussed. I steeled my heart against the boyish innocence of his face. They say the Boston Strangler was a picture of boyish innocence. I picked up a pen and started tapping the desk.

"Victoria?"

Thoughts ran like crazy through my mind. Should I? What would he do if I confronted him alone? But at least the seniors weren't here to get hurt. I should probably wait for Benjamin, though. I'd tried to call him a couple of times with still no answer.

"I'm sorry, Corky. I have tons of work to catch up with. I'll talk to the seniors later." I mustered up a smile. "Don't sweat it. I'm sure it's nothing serious." Maybe that would pacify his suspicions for now.

He tightened his lips and spun around, his back stiff. From aggravation? Or was it anger?

The clock in the great hall chimed ten and, once again, filled me with dread. Fear rippled down my back. Was I safe here with Corky? What if he figured out I knew the truth? I wished Buster were inside, but I'd instructed Corky earlier to leave him to run and play in the backyard. At the moment, however, I needed the reassurance of his presence more than he needed fresh air and exercise.

I stood and almost tiptoed to the front door. Slipping quietly through, I went around back and called softly for Buster. He came running with his tail wagging ninety miles an hour

I bent over and rubbed his head, putting up with his kisses. "Hello, boy. Glad to see me? Well, I'm just as glad to see you. Come on. Keep me company." Buster followed me around to the porch where I sat on the step, not caring as dampness soaked the seat of my pants. He bolted across the yard and was back in a moment with a ball he'd retrieved from the bushes. I tossed it too near the street, and Mrs. Miller, driving by in her bright red SUV, threw me a cheery wave. Apparently she'd forgotten she was mad at us all. I waved back.

Maybe she was nosy and gossipy, but she'd been a neighbor for many years.

Corky's Ford pickup backed out of the garage. What is it with men and their trucks? They have to have them even if they live smack in the middle of a city. Corky rolled down his window. "I have to go get apples. Do you need anything from the store?"

I replied in the negative, and he rolled up the window and pulled out of the drive.

Too restless to work, I decided a few minutes of solitaire might help me relax. I was still playing an hour later when the front door crashed open. "Victoria!" Miss Georgina's shrill voice pierced the air, and suddenly she and Miss Jane rushed into my office, gushing with relief when they saw me.

"Oh, thank the Lord, Victoria," Miss Georgina gasped, clutching her chest.

Miss Jane nodded. "We thought you were dead."

Miss Evalina and the men entered the room.

"We told them not to get all riled up," said Frank.

"But, as usual," Martin sneered, "they wouldn't listen."

I glanced at Miss Evalina, who stood with an expression of relief on her face.

"Why in the world would you think I was dead?"

Miss Evalina ran her hand across her forehead, a sure sign she'd been worried, too. "We didn't go to church, Victoria. We wanted to stay together. We've been at the Mocha Java all morning trying to make sense of everything. But we decided you shouldn't be here alone with Corky, so we came on home. When we saw his truck was missing, we thought he might have . . ." She stopped.

Understanding dawned on me, and I stood up and hurried around my desk to put my arm around her. "Thank you all for caring so much. As you can see, I'm fine." I put my other arm around Miss Georgina and reached my hand to Miss Jane. Together, we walked to the parlor, and when they were all seated I went to make tea.

As I waited for the kettle to boil, I tried to get some semblance of order in my thoughts. Should I confront Corky or wait for Benjamin? But where was he and why didn't he answer his phone? We had to find Miss Aggie. Was she alive and well? There'd been no sign of her or her car. Or so the sheriff said. Was she lying somewhere injured? The thoughts slammed at my brain, and my head pounded. I simply would not wait any longer. But what about the seniors? Would I be placing them in danger? Maybe I should send them on an errand.

I slapped my head. No. They weren't senile. They were as capable as I was. Maybe more so. The kettle squealed and I made the tea, placing the pot on the tea cart with the cups, saucers, cream, and sugar. The heady fragrance of bergamot wafted from the Earl Grey. The tiny silver spoons weren't in their usual place, so I grabbed some plastic stirrers from the drawer by the stove.

The kitchen door opened behind me, and I jumped and whirled around.

Corky set his grocery bags on the counter. "Sorry if I startled you. Here, I'll take the cart in for you."

"No," I said, a little too shortly. "I mean, thank you, Corky, but I can get it. Why don't you put the groceries away and join us in the great hall?" Somehow, the parlor seemed a little too cozy for the confrontation ahead of us.

He nodded, and I wheeled the cart to the hallway and stopped to enter the vast, dark great hall. There was no fire, but it wasn't as cold today. The heating system should give us enough warmth, even in this mammoth room. It had to be at least fifty degrees or more for the ice and snow to thaw so quickly. I turned on the lights and then wheeled the tea cart into the parlor. I'd give them their choice. They could stay here and have their tea, leave the house while I talked to Corky, or join us.

The sky had clouded over again, and an almost medieval ambience pervaded the great hall. The lights from the chandelier lit the very center of the vast room, and the wall sconces gave just enough light to cast shadows to the corners of the massive hall. A pity I couldn't knock out some walls for windows to let more light in. But I had no intention of making such drastic changes to the original structure.

We waited in silence. I inhaled Miss Evalina's

faint lavender scent and was grateful there was no watermelon mixed with honeysuckle to overwhelm me today. Martin tapped his foot on the hardwood floor. His feet looked huge next to Miss Jane's. I jerked my attention away from his size-twelve shoes and watched Miss Georgina pull at a tiny loose thread on her sweater. The somber faces of my friends nearly made me call the whole thing off. But it was too late for that. I was determined to find out what Corky knew about Miss Aggie's whereabouts.

The door to the foyer opened, and Corky stood framed by the massive oak door. He closed it behind him and came into the room, stopping in front of me.

"What's wrong? Why does everyone look so glum?" he asked with a slight chuckle; then his face stilled. "Is there news?"

"Sit down, Corky." I motioned to a large wing-back chair. He complied, with a puzzled expression on his face.

"Or should I say Dane?" I gazed intently at him as shock registered on his face and he paled.

I waited while he licked his lips. I wondered if he'd deny it, even now.

"Victoria, I can explain."

"Please do," I said.

He stood and began to pace, stopping once more in front of my chair.

"All right, as you obviously know, my name is

Dane Pennington. My grandfather was Aunt Aggie's brother, Forrest." He paused, and when no one spoke, he continued. "I grew up hearing about Pennington House, or as my grandfather used to jokingly say, Pennington Castle." He inhaled deeply and sat back down, leaning forward. "To a young boy of modest means, it sounded like a magical kingdom. I know Gramps probably embellished, but my head was in the clouds from the time I was four or five years old."

Losing patience, I stood and clenched my fists. "Where's Miss Aggie? If you've hurt her . . ."

He closed his eyes and tension tightened his face. "I haven't. I promise you. I knew you'd think that if you found out I was a Pennington. Please, just hear me out."

I felt a tug on my sleeve and looked down at Miss Evalina. She gave a little shake of her head. She was right, of course. I wouldn't get any information out of him this way. I sat back down. "Go ahead, then, but make it fast."

"Aunt Aggie visited us once after my grandfather passed away. I must have been ten or eleven. I felt like I was meeting a queen. By that time, we were living in Jefferson City, in the house inherited from my maternal grandparents. Dad had made me promise not to ask questions about the family history and the house, but I had to force myself to keep that promise. I wrote her a letter full of questions when I was fourteen or fifteen, and she may have thought that indicated I wanted money or something from her. I didn't. I just needed to know."

He took a long drink of water from the bottle he'd brought in with him. "I'm not sure if it was the letter or something else, but we didn't hear from her much after that. Dad tried, but after a while he sort of gave up. I blamed myself, but I never did tell him about the letter." He swallowed and inhaled deeply. "When I was in my last year of culinary school, I read an article about a man named Jacque St. Leger who'd converted an old castle into a hotel and restaurant. The accompanying picture intrigued me, and I thought of Pennington House standing there empty and probably going to ruins. I knew better than to write Aunt Aggie about it. She'd think I wanted her to deed it to me. What I really wanted was to buy it, but I had no idea how I'd come up with that kind of money."

Frank stood and shook his finger in Corky's face. "So you changed your mind and tried to con Aggie out of it, is that it?"

I cringed. Had Corky managed to talk his aunt Aggie into leaving Pennington House to him and then gotten rid of her?

Corky put his head in his hands. "No! That's not what happened."

Miss Evalina reached up and touched Frank's hand. He looked down at her with frustration but flung himself back down, muttering under his breath. I was surprised to see Miss Evalina's face register sympathy as she gazed at Corky. "Go ahead, Corky," she said, "tell us the rest."

Corky pulled a handkerchief from his pocket and blew his nose loudly. It was only then I noticed his eyes swam with tears.

"Okay." He took another deep breath before he continued. "I started making plans. Dad and Mom knew I wanted to go to Europe, so they bought my plane ticket. I worked my way across Europe, visiting inns, castles, and anything else I thought might inspire me. In Paris I even took some advanced French culinary classes. And I met Jacque St. Leger. He was a famous restaurateur, owning a number of fine restaurants all over France, including the one I'd seen in the magazine."

He took another drink from his water bottle. I found myself pulled into his story, holding my breath as I waited for him to continue. I cleared my throat and sat up straight. I wanted Corky to have a good explanation, but I couldn't forget the purpose of this conversation.

"St. Leger was interested in my idea about Pennington House. I showed him pictures I'd drawn and photos I'd collected during my travels. He left on a business trip just before I left Paris, but we agreed to keep in touch.

"When I came back to the states, I got a position in an elite Kansas City restaurant. I was informed, even with my credentials, I'd have to start as an apprentice chef. I had no problem with that. Within three months I'd been promoted to banquet sous chef and a year later to executive sous chef, which means I was executive assistant to the executive chef." He stopped and looked at each of us. "I suppose you don't really care about all that. But what it basically meant was in order to go higher, I'd have had to look for a position elsewhere, because the executive chef wasn't going anywhere. I didn't want to go to another restaurant, and besides, I still had my dream." He rubbed his hand across the back of his neck.

"St. Leger and I kept in touch. Last year he came to the states on business, and we met for dinner in New York City. He asked me if I still had plans to convert Pennington House. If so, would I be interested in a partner? We flew to Springfield and rented a car then drove up to the estate to look around the exterior of the place. We looked through the first-floor windows then found a ladder in an outbuilding. With that, we managed to get a pretty good idea of the second floor, although we couldn't see higher than that."

Corky paused and looked at me intently. "Even in its state of neglect and disrepair, the possibilities were obvious. I could almost see it in its former grandeur. St. Leger was impressed and offered to back me for a large portion of the purchase, repair, and renovation, as well as a good share of the overhead for the first year of business. I'd invest also, plus oversee the work and run the establishment, so we'd be equal partners."

He stopped, and I could see the reluctance in his eyes. I shivered. Almost afraid to hear what would come next.

"I knew Aunt Aggie would likely throw me out on my ear if I approached her with the idea. According to my grandfather, he'd tried for years to get her to sell the place, but she refused. It seems there was some sort of feud. My grandfather said she was stubborn and preferred to let the mansion go to ruin rather than let him have his way about anything."

I remembered the entry in Miss Aggie's diary about the shady characters who wanted the mansion, but I didn't see any reason to mention it to Corky. Who knew the real story behind it?

"I decided to come to Cedar Chapel to check things out. It was unlikely Aunt Aggie would recognize me as long as it had been since she'd seen me. So I came and rented an apartment with an assumed name." He looked uncomfortable and slightly guilty. "Actually, my grandfather always called me a corker when I was small, and my older sister used to tease me and called me Corky. The last name was my mom's maiden name."

"So, what did you plan to do after you lied about your name, young man?" Miss Jane snapped.

Corky's face flamed. "Actually, I had no idea. But the first night I was here, I saw Victoria's ad in the paper. It seemed like the perfect solution."

A chill went through me. A perfect solution for what? Murder?

19

An ominous silence filled the room. My heart jumped as the grandfather clock tolled the hour. Was it louder than usual or simply my overwrought imagination playing tricks with my mind?

Corky's deep sigh was audible in the deathly quiet of the room. With determination, I steeled myself against his pleading glance.

He blinked his eyes as if waking from a dream.

"The last couple of weeks before Aunt Aggie disappeared, I caught her watching me, and I knew it was only a matter of time before she figured out who I was. Then one night she followed me out to my car and demanded an explanation. She had finally recognized me." He shrugged. "I think it was the curls that did it."

So Miss Aggie had confronted her nephew, Dane Pennington, shortly before she disappeared. I could feel the tension in the room, taut like an elastic band, pulling tighter and tighter till finally it was near the breaking point.

"I think we've heard enough, Corky," I said. My voice sounded hoarse, unnatural to me. "Do you want to turn yourself in, or shall I call Sheriff Turner myself?"

His eyes widened, and a choking sound shot from his throat. "No. You don't understand. It wasn't like that."

Miss Evalina reached over and touched my arm. "Let him finish his story, Victoria."

Relief crossed his face as I reluctantly nodded for him to continue.

"She asked me to come back later when everyone was in bed. It must have been eleven that night when I got back, and we sat in the kitchen until two or three the next morning, drinking tea and talking. I decided to be honest and tell her why I was there, thinking she'd be furious and probably wake the whole house up." He shook his head and smiled slightly. "To my surprise and delight, she was excited when I told her my ideas for Pennington House. Oh, she told me off good for not telling her who I was from the beginning, but she said she understood my concern."

Miss Jane's eyes had widened, an expression of disbelief on her face. "Do you mean to tell me Aggie agreed to turn Pennington House into a hotel and restaurant?"

"Yes, ma'am. Well, she wasn't sure at first. In the beginning she thought I was trying to scam her, but when she realized I wanted to buy the place and was willing to pay well, she started to change her mind. The night before she disappeared, she told me she wanted to be a partner. And she wanted to be smack in the middle of everything. Even had some ideas of her own. I was really surprised at how much she knew about the hotel and restaurant business. Still am."

"Why, that explains why Aggie was getting on the Internet and her sudden interest in inns and bed-and-breakfast establishments." Miss Georgina's voice rang with excitement.

"You may be right. If the story is true." Because as plausible as it sounded, it might just be a well-thought-out pack of lies.

Corky's face grew serious again. "The next day, when she disappeared, I thought she'd changed her mind again and left to avoid me. It even crossed my mind the rest of you could be in on it. But when you called the sheriff, I knew you were in the dark, too. I still thought she might have gone somewhere to think things out, but when I heard her jewels were missing, I knew something was wrong." He cleared his throat then continued. "Hoping it was a mistake, I started searching for them. I'd been looking through her things for possible leads when you caught me upstairs that day."

Frank leaned forward and eyed Corky. "Yeah, well, that's a pretty good story you're spinning, mister, but there's one very important item I'd like for you to explain."

Corky sent a questioning look Frank's way. "What is it, Frank? I'll try to answer any questions you have."

"Well then, maybe you'll tell us why you were going from pawn shop to pawn shop for two weeks straight? You even hit the ones in Springfield."

A pained expression crossed Corky's face. "So that's why you've given me the third degree for the past couple of weeks." He sighed. "Two reasons. When I heard the jewels had disappeared, I thought if I could trace them, it might lead us to whoever abducted Aunt Aggie. You see, I happen to have a stack of old pictures that belonged to my grand-father, Forrest. One of them was a photo of the diamond pieces, so I took it around to all the pawn shops in the area. No one had seen them, though. Or at least no one admitted it."

I glanced at Miss Evalina and suddenly we avoided each other's eyes. I, for one, was thinking about the film lying snug as a bug in the safe in my office.

Martin spoke up. "I don't know about anyone else, Corky, but I believe you."

"Yes," Miss Evalina said with an emphatic nod. "I'm inclined to believe you, too."

Miss Georgina gasped, and fear crossed her face.

"Georgina, what's wrong?" Miss Jane reached over and grabbed her hand.

Her voice was weak. "Aggie may have gone to Pennington House."

"What do you mean?" I asked. "Why would you think she'd go there?"

"She's always been impulsive. In her excitement about the hotel, it would be just like her to take off without telling anyone and go look the place over. What if she fell or had an attack of some sort?"

Astonishment and fear were written on the faces of all the old friends as realization dawned.

I jumped up. "Get your coats. You'll need to show me the way." Feet scurried as the seniors rushed to their rooms for coats and hats. I grabbed a heavy old sweater from the hook next to the kitchen door. By the time I'd slipped into it and turned, Corky had shrugged into his jacket.

"No, Corky," He stopped in surprise and I softened my voice. "I need you to be here in case Benjamin calls. In fact, I'd like for you to keep trying his number. Tell him where we've gone."

"But, Victoria, she's my aunt."

"I know. But I need someone here, and I don't think anyone can talk Miss Aggie's friends into staying behind."

A disappointed expression crossed his face. "You still aren't sure about me, are you?"

Warmth flooded my face. "I'm sorry. I wish I could say I was."

He nodded shortly then reached into his jacket pocket and tossed me his cell phone. "Here, you may need this."

Surprised, I caught it and slipped it into the deep sweater pocket. "Thanks. I wish things were different."

"I understand. You're thinking of Aunt Aggie as well as the others. I don't blame you. Should

I call Sheriff Turner and ask him to meet you at Pennington House?"

I bit my lip and thought about it. "No. There's no reason to think he'll suddenly take us seriously. If we need him, I'll call him from your cell phone."

Corky nodded, but the expression on his face was decidedly worried. Maybe I should bring him along. I tightened my resolve and stepped into the garage, where the seniors waited in the van.

Before I inserted the key in the ignition, I bowed my head. "Lord, only You know what we'll find at Pennington House. Please be with us and make us strong. Give us wisdom. In Jesus' name. Amen."

Amens resounded from the rear of the van and from Miss Evalina, who sat beside me. As I backed out into the street, I could hear a murmur as Miss Georgina continued to pray.

"Which is the best way to get there?" I asked, realizing I might have pointed the van in the wrong direction.

"Go to the road where we found Buster, and we'll direct you from there," Miss Jane instructed.

Complying, I drove through town and turned onto the narrow, blacktopped road. After what seemed like hours, but couldn't have been more than thirty minutes, I asked, "Keep going?"

"Yes." Miss Evalina's voice cracked, and I feared her nerves were strung as tight as mine. "Go past the last house we visited before, and we'll tell you where to turn."

I drove on for what seemed an eternity, finally passing the house where the cat beat up Buster. Another mile went by, then, "Turn right onto that dirt road just ahead, Victoria." Miss Evalina had leaned forward and was almost on the edge of her seat.

The ladies in back had leaned forward, too, and looked over our shoulders as we turned onto the narrow, dusty road. "This brings back memories," Miss Jane said. At her nostalgic tone, a strange feeling ran through my body. These ladies had been down this road together many times when they were young. I felt as though I might round a bend and drive right into a past I'd had no part of.

The road wound up a steep hill. As we rounded a curve, I gasped, and awe washed over me. About a half mile farther up, a three-story brick mansion stood regally on top of the hill. I'd only seen the chimneys before, and the sight of the old mansion almost took my breath away.

As we pulled into the circular, weed-overgrown drive, excitement mixed with dread bubbled up in my stomach.

"That's Aggie's car!" Frank exclaimed. He jumped out of the van before it stopped rolling.

A light blue '93 Taurus GL stood in the knee-high grass at the far side of the mansion. It was either Miss Aggie's or its twin.

Seat belts released, and we hurried out of the van and started toward the front porch.

"Wait a minute!" At the tone of Martin's voice we all stopped. "Why in thunder would Aggie pull her car all the way over there?"

I glanced nervously around. Martin was right. Maybe we'd better . . .

The front door of the mansion opened, and Junior Whitly stood in the doorway, a rifle on his shoulder, obviously sighted on one of us. He moved forward slowly and motioned us toward him. "Don't try anything, now. My trigger finger is mighty jumpy."

Frank put his arm protectively around Miss Evalina and glanced at me. I stepped forward reluctantly. The important thing was to keep everyone safe. We filed into the huge foyer, and the rifle-wielding abductor kicked the door shut.

The foyer opened into a massive room with a wide staircase, reminiscent of Twelve Oaks from *Gone with the Wind.* However, the floor and banisters were covered with dust, and trash lay scattered all over the place. A card table with some rusty metal chairs sat against one wall, covered with papers and fast-food containers. I didn't see anyone but Junior.

"What've you done with Miss Aggie?" I snapped and then clamped my mouth shut as I realized that might not be very smart.

He squinted at me through pale blue eyes and

sneered. "You'll see her soon enough. Get on up the stairs."

I looked at him intently, wondering if I could grab the gun, but decided he'd shoot me before I got anywhere near him. I led the way as we scampered up the tall staircase with him following along with the rifle.

"The barrel of this here rifle's pressed against Martin's back, so don't try anything stupid." I glanced around and saw he wasn't kidding. He was on the step behind Martin with the gun pressed against him. At the top of the stairs, he directed us to continue up the next flight of steps. When we reached the landing for the third floor, he motioned us down to the end of the hall, where he shoved Martin aside and unlocked a door on the left. He kept the rifle aimed at us, stifling my urge to try to jump him.

We filed into the room, and he slammed the door behind us.

Anger overcame my sense, and I hammered on the door. "Junior Whitly, you'd better let us out of here!"

"Jane! Eva! Oh, you're all here. You've come to rescue me." At the sound of Miss Aggie's voice I whirled around. She stumbled across the floor and fell into Miss Evalina's arms. As the others crowded around her, I stood back and ran my eyes over her from top to bottom. Her dress was dirty and wrinkled and white roots grew from her scalp. So much for the wonder of coal black tresses. But she didn't appear hurt in any way, although I couldn't know for sure at first glance.

I grabbed Corky's cell phone from my pocket and punched in 9-1-1. To my consternation, the phone was dead.

"No signal here probably," Frank observed.

Frustrated, I looked around the room, hoping to find a way out. I was surprised to find it fairly neat and clean, although a slight odor of stale perfume clung to the air. A sturdy sofa stood against one wall, with a blanket folded neatly on the end. A fluffy pillow topped the blanket. Nearby stood a small table with a mug and a case of bottled water on top and a wooden chair pushed up underneath. A small trash can held a take-out box and several crumpled-up bags and napkins. It seemed as if Miss Aggie had at least been allowed to eat and sleep.

The ladies crowded around her while Frank and Martin both fired off questions. Miss Aggie appeared confused as she looked from one to the other.

"All right, folks, let her breathe at least." I stepped forward and took her hand. "Miss Aggie, we're so happy to see you. Have you been harmed in any way?"

She inhaled deeply and closed her eyes for a second. "No, my dear, I'm unharmed. Let's sit down and I'll tell you all what happened." The four elderly ladies crowded together on the sofa, and Frank pulled the lone chair over for me. Then he and Martin hunkered down beside me.

"How is Corky?" Miss Aggie asked, looking at me a little fearfully.

"Corky's fine. We know he's your relative. Did he have anything to do with this?"

"Oh, I knew if you found out about him you'd think he'd killed me or something. No. Absolutely not." An emphatic shake of her head let me know I could lay down that suspicion. "Did he tell you his plans for Pennington House?"

"He sure did," Miss Jane said. "Did you really agree to the hotel and restaurant?"

"Yes, I did. Don't you think it's a smashing idea?" Miss Aggie's face glowed, and her voice sang with excitement.

I shook my head at her apparent unconcern about our situation. "Yes, Miss Aggie. If you think it's smashing, so do I."

"Well, I was so caught up in the idea, I decided to drive over here." Miss Aggie sighed. "Guess it wasn't such a good idea."

"It was a terrible idea. Why didn't you tell someone where you were going?" Now that Miss Aggie appeared to be all right, Miss Jane's voice shook with anger.

Miss Aggie reached over and patted her friend's hand. "Calm down, Jane. I didn't say anything because I wanted to be sure it was a legitimate business arrangement first. After all, I've been fooled before where money is concerned, and I didn't want to look like a fool again."

"What happened, Miss Aggie? Is Junior one of the bank robbers?" Even as I asked, I thought the answer was fairly obvious.

"Yes, they showed up a few minutes after I arrived. Apparently Taylor heard me talking about Pennington House in the coffee shop one day and realized it would be a good place to use as headquarters from which to pull their robberies. It makes a good hideout, since it's been abandoned for so long."

Miss Evalina's eyes narrowed. "So, Taylor's involved, too, of course."

"Naturally. You know Junior wouldn't be anywhere without big brother. Taylor's led Junior into trouble for years, but nothing this bad before. It seems their business hasn't been doing well. They were about to lose it. So Taylor and his friend thought up their scheme and, of course, Junior got pulled into it, too."

Frank coughed. "So they aren't in this alone?"

"There's one more. They call him Jake. I don't know who he is, but I think he'd have killed me the first day, if not for Junior and Taylor. They always did like me. I suppose because they knew I liked them, too." She sighed. "But they couldn't stop him from taking my diamonds."

"But, Aggie." Jane cast a puzzled look at her friend. "You weren't wearing your diamonds when you left that day."

"They were under my clothes. You don't think I'd flaunt them for anyone to see, do you?" Miss Aggie snorted. "If that man was any kind of gentleman, they never would have found them."

She cast a sideways glance at Martin and Frank. "Would you allow me a moment with the ladies alone, please?"

When the men had walked to the other side of the room, Miss Aggie leaned forward and whispered, "Are my roots showing?"

At our silence, she groaned.

"Here, Aggie." Miss Georgina reached inside her huge handbag and pulled out the wool scarf she'd worn around her neck when the weather was colder.

We helped Miss Aggie until every piece of white was covered, then, blushing, she motioned the men back over.

Martin looked amused, and I sent him a warning look. He ducked his head and coughed.

"Is that a truck I hear?" Frank asked.

"They're back," Miss Aggie said. "Be careful. I'm not sure what Jake will do when he sees all of you."

A few minutes later I heard loud footsteps coming up the stairs then down the hall. A key turned in the lock, and the door flew open.

The man who stood there was of medium height and wiry, with a mane of black curls. The look of malevolence he shot us caused my stomach to lurch with fear. Even more than the revolver he held in his hand.

The gun loomed large and menacing as Jake waved it wildly, cursing and screaming at Junior Whitley, who cowered in the background.

"Did you even bother to search them, you idiot?" He turned quickly, backhanded Junior, then spun around, his eyes darting from one of us to another.

Junior gulped and his face paled. "S–s–sorry, Jake. I didn't think about it. They're just a bunch of old people and a girl."

Jake spun again and glared at the trembling Junior. "Did it ever occur to you they might be bugged, you nitwit?"

Another slap threw Junior against the wall across the hallway. I knew I had to do something. Maybe I could grab Jake from behind while his attention was on his partner. Then we could all overpower him. I took a step forward. Jake whirled and stepped in front of me before I could move again. He slapped me. My neck snapped back. I landed against the table, and pain shot through my spine and ribs.

Miss Aggie slipped her arm around me on one side, and Miss Evalina put her hand on my other shoulder. Out of the corner of my eye, I saw movement. *No, Frank, don't try it.* Jake saw the motion, too, and yelled as he waved the gun at Frank. I knew I needed to move while he was distracted. Keeping my eye on Jake, I slipped the phone from my pocket into Miss Aggie's. She glanced at me out of the corner of her eye and gave a quick nod. Maybe there would be a signal later.

Footsteps sounded on the stairs, and a voice yelled, "Jake, did you hit my brother?"

"Yeah, I hit the sniveling little creep. You got something to say about it?"

The man that appeared in the doorway was an older carbon copy of Junior except for the bandage on his hand. "I've told you and told you. I ain't gonna stand for you knocking Junior around."

"Well, maybe you'd better teach him a few things. Like how to use his brain. Now, do you want to search these people or hold the gun?"

Taylor glanced at Miss Evalina, and when I saw the expression on his face, I knew we were in big trouble. Jake wouldn't be easily talked out of murder this time. Taylor searched Frank and Martin, then with a grimace, he turned to Miss Evalina. "Sorry, Miz Swayne. I gotta search you." She stood stock-still and stared at him while his uninjured hand grazed her clothing. Next he searched Miss Jane and Miss Georgina then me. He found the keys to the van right away and crammed them into his jeans pocket. I fought the urge to slug him as his fingers whisked down my sides. Instead, I stared at him until he averted his eyes.

"They're clean." He stepped back toward the door.

"What about her?" Jake pointed his gun at Miss Aggie.

"We've already searched her, Jake. Remember?"

"Well, I can see you aren't much smarter than that idiot brother of yours. Don't you think someone may have slipped something to her, thinking we wouldn't search her?"

I groaned. Apparently Jake was smarter than he looked.

"I need to go to the ladies' room," Miss Aggie piped up.

Jake's sneer indicated that ploy wouldn't work. "You can wait a minute. Then I might let you go to the can."

Taylor stepped in front of Miss Aggie and searched her. When he reached into her pocket, his mouth dropped open and his eyes widened. He held up the cell phone.

"Uh-huh? Didn't I tell you?" Jake snapped. "You can't take anything for granted. Now come on downstairs. We need to talk." He shot another menacing look in our direction as they stomped out.

I heard the sound of the key turning. Locked in, again.

Ten minutes later the door creaked open and

Taylor walked in, gun in hand. He nodded to Miss Aggie. "I guess you can go to the bathroom now. Then everyone's coming downstairs."

Miss Georgina gasped, and Miss Jane looked as frightened as I felt.

"I don't need to go anymore." Miss Aggie looked intently at her ex-student. "You wouldn't let anyone hurt us, would you, Taylor?"

A wild look filled his eyes, and he looked away.

"Taylor?" she insisted.

"Miss Aggie, I'll try my best to keep you safe," he said. "But Jake's about gone ballistic that so many of you have seen us. It would've been better for you if your friends hadn't shown up."

We walked down the stairs two by two with Taylor following closely behind. I was relieved they were moving us to the first floor. There would have been no chance of escape from the third-floor room. When we reached the bottom of the stairs, he directed us to a room off the foyer, then closed and locked the door behind us.

Miss Aggie sauntered around the empty room. She ran her fingers over the mantel, then wrinkling her nose, removed a hanky from her pocket and wiped her hand. "This was the reception/waiting room my father used for business. His office was through that connecting door." She walked over and tried the doorknob, but it refused to turn.

I ran to the front window and pulled aside the heavy drapes, creating a cloud of dust. I coughed as my lungs and throat filled with the particles. I stepped back for a moment until I could breathe again and then peered through the dirty pane. For the first time, I noticed thick woods blocked the road leading up to the house. Good. When we got away, we'd be on foot, and it would be easier to escape our captors if we made our way through the thick foliage of the enormous oak and walnut trees. Miss Georgina clutched Miss Evalina's sleeve and whimpered. "Eva, are they going to kill us?"

Miss Evalina put her arm around the plump shoulders and gave her a squeeze. "We'll be fine. But it's time we prayed. We should have done so when Junior first locked us in that room."

We bowed our heads and Miss Evalina called on God with sincerity and trust. I don't know if the others felt better afterward, but somehow I knew He'd heard Miss Evalina's prayer, and a rush of hope based on faith rather than the anger and adrenaline that had been moving me rose up in my heart. And with the hope, determination.

Apparently, Frank had received a dose of the same. "Okay," he said. "I believe God answers prayer, but maybe we need to try to figure out a way to free ourselves. Aggie, isn't there a tunnel under this house?"

"Yes, but it won't do us any good. The hidden panel is in the library down the hall."

"Well, let's try the windows, then." Frank and

Martin made several attempts to open the ancient windows, but they remained frozen in place. "You'll never be able to get through the window, Frank. My father built them too sturdy."

Frank ignored her. "We could break them easily enough, but not while those lunatics are standing by the door. They'd be in here with their guns before we could all get out." He walked over to the door and began to examine it.

"You'd never be able to break down that door, Frank. It's too thick."

I wished Miss Aggie would leave him alone. She wasn't helping anything. Let him try to come up with a solution, even if only in his own mind. Frank was a protector by nature. If we didn't find a way out of here, I knew he'd die trying to protect Miss Evalina and the rest of us. The room was getting darker, and I suspected we didn't have a lot of time. I took Frank aside.

"We're going to have to chance breaking the window," I whispered.

"I know, but have you noticed the type of window it is?"

"Yeah, leaded with small panes."

"There's no way Georgina or I could squeeze through there, and I'm not sure about the rest of them. The frame is too sturdy for us to break without some kind of instrument."

"Okay, we just need a plan. There's got to be a way out of here."

At that moment I glanced toward the window and thought I saw a shadow dart around the side of the house. I hurried over and, peering through, saw a man's form follow closely behind the other. Was that . . . ?

I turned and motioned for the others to draw closer. "Someone just crept around the house," I whispered. "It looked like Benjamin, but I'm not sure."

Understanding and hope dawned on each face. Silently we tiptoed to the door and strained to listen. I could barely make out the sound of voices. As the murmur rose, it sounded like our captors were locked in a heated argument. A shiver ran through me at the thought they were probably discussing how to do away with us.

Time seemed to stand still as we waited.

"Are you sure you didn't imagine it?" Martin asked.

"No, I saw something. Of course, for all I know it could have been more of their friends joining them." I wished I'd thought of that before getting everyone's hopes up.

Frank snorted. "If it's friends of theirs, why would they sneak around?" He had a very good point, and once more a surge of hope rose to push away the fear.

But then . . . A thread of worry niggled its way into my mind.

"If it's Benjamin, I wish I knew if someone was

with him. What if he gets hurt trying to rescue us?"

"Benjamin knows what he's doing. And seeing there's only one way he could know where we are, I imagine Corky is with him."

"Okay, but I'm not going to let them walk into a trap."

I removed my heavy sweater and started to wrap it around my arm.

"Wait a minute, let me do that." Frank took the sweater and wrapped it around his own arm.

"What are you doing, Frank?" Georgina looked ready to faint.

"He's going to break the window and help Victoria squeeze through." Miss Evalina smiled encouragingly. "She's the only one who might fit."

"Good idea." Miss Jane glowed at Frank, then at me.

"Listen, I'll find Ben and Corky and tell them where to find you."

"But what if that's not Ben out there?" Martin piped up.

"Then I'll find something to smash this window frame with and get you out of here."

At that moment, Frank hit the window pane hard and it smashed, sending shards all over the floor. He knocked large shards from around the pane, and I crawled through. He gave a shove, and I was on the ground.

Not waiting to see if the robbers had heard the smashing glass, I ran in the direction Benjamin, or so I hoped, had disappeared.

As I passed the front porch, I heard a crash.

"Let's get out of here!" Taylor's shout sounded clearly through the heavy front door.

"Taylor, help! He's got me!" That was Junior.

Excitement rushed through me as I bounded up the steps.

A heavy thud sounded then another loud crash. I heard Jake's loud curse, then nothing.

The wail of a siren filled the silence. I rushed off the porch as two patrol cars squealed to a stop in front of the house.

Sheriff Turner, Tom Lewis, and the FBI agent jumped out of one car and shoved past me, rushing to the door, guns drawn. Three officers I didn't know piled out of the other car and spread out behind them. "Open up, it's the law." The sheriff aimed at the lock, but before he could fire, the door flew open and the men rushed in. Voices rang out from different parts of the house, calling our names. "Victoria! Where are you?"

I ran back onto the porch and rushed through the door.

"Corky, they're in here." Benjamin stood at the door to the reception room with a crowbar in his hand.

"Wait, Benjamin!" Corky shouted. "Don't use the crowbar! Aunt Aggie, are you in there?"

"I'm here, Dane. You should find all the house keys on one of those men. They took them away from me."

Benjamin whirled around and stopped as he saw me standing there.

A moment later I was in his arms.

"I'm all right. Go help the others."

At that moment, the seniors all rushed out the door and into the foyer, led by Miss Aggie.

"We suspected Corky all along, you see." Sheriff Turner's voice sounded a little sheepish as he sat in the chair behind his desk and explained to us.

"Then why didn't you tell us?" I demanded, indignation rising up inside me.

"We're not in the habit of telling a civilian everything about an investigation," Tom said. "Anyway, we figured you'd let the cat out of the bag." He grinned. "Turns out there wasn't any cat in that particular bag."

Sheriff Turner's face flamed, and he threw a look of disgust at Tom. "Yeah, we were headed down the wrong trail, it seems."

"Well," said Miss Evalina, ever gracious, "we took the same trail, Bob. I'm glad we were wrong."

"We found out Corky was Dane Pennington the day after Miss Aggie disappeared," the sheriff continued, "but had no evidence at all against him. We followed him and drew the same conclusion you did, Frank, about the pawn shops."

Corky chose that moment to speak up. "While I don't especially like being talked about as though

I'm not here, not to mention being suspected of robbery and murder, I'm sure glad you followed me today."

"Well, I'd say you and Benjamin pretty near had them under control, but I'm glad we got there in time to help round them up." The look on Sheriff Turner's face was sheer satisfaction. He cleared his throat and looked straight at me.

"What?" Confusion tightened my stomach as I tried to decipher his shadowed look.

"I know I gave you a hard time. When we put your cook on our suspect list, we didn't know who else might be involved with him."

"Well, thanks a lot, Sheriff. You've only known me since I was a baby."

"I was just doing my job. I had to be sure."

"All right," I said, softening. "I agree. What's important is that Miss Aggie is safe and sound. Now if I can just convince the other ladies to come home, maybe we'll all get some rest tonight."

When the doctor had said, over Miss Aggie's protests, that she had to stay in the hospital overnight for observation, the other ladies insisted on staying with her. I hoped by now they were tired enough to go home.

We left, Corky following us in Benjamin's truck, and drove to the hospital, where we found Miss Aggie, propped up on pillows and wide awake, surrounded by her friends.

"Victoria, we found out about Buster's gunshot

wound." Miss Jane's face glowed with excitement. "Tell her, Aggie."

Miss Aggie's eyes were bright as she glanced at me. "When I was driving to Pennington House, I saw this dog walking along the side of the road. You all know how I can't stand to see an animal abandoned. I stopped, and he seemed so happy to see me, licking my face and wagging his tail. I looked to see if he had a collar. He didn't, so I let him jump into the backseat." She stopped to take a breath. "When I got to the house, I let him out. When the men accosted me, I slapped him on the rump and he took off. But one of them shot at him. I didn't know they'd hit him." Her face crumpled.

"Well, he's fat and sassy and having a wonderful time now, Miss Aggie." I patted her shoulder. "I'll bet he's going to be glad to see you."

Miss Aggie brightened and finally submitted to a sleeping pill. Then she lay back on her pillow and was soon snoring loudly.

"I think maybe I'll go home after all," Miss Georgina said, covering a yawn with the back of her dainty hand.

Miss Evalina stood. "We may as well all go. Aggie will be knocked out until morning anyway."

Miss Jane nodded. "I'm more tired than I thought."

An hour later the lodge had settled down for the

night as all the boarders had gone to bed. Benjamin and I leaned back in the porch swing and gazed at the stars that dotted the heavens. Peace filled my heart as he held my hand in his.

"I found my faith, Vickie."

I could feel my face glow as I smiled at him.

"When I knew you were in trouble, I cried out to Him and suddenly faith was there. I knew you'd be okay."

"Oh, Benjamin. That's the most wonderful news you could tell me. It was worth it all, to hear this."

He bent down and kissed me on the nose.

I giggled. "That tickles."

"So, when did you first know you loved me?" A shiver of excitement coursed up my arm as he rubbed his thumb over my fingers.

"What makes you think I love you, Benjamin Grant?"

He grinned. "Oh, because I couldn't love anyone who didn't love me back."

A smile tugged at the corners of my lips. Two could play this game. "So, when did *you* first know you loved *me?*"

"When I spray-painted Sparky, of course."

"What?" I turned around to face him. "That was a fine way to show love."

He laughed. "But that was the point. I couldn't risk having you find out."

"Hmm. I probably would have made your life

miserable, at that," I answered with a smirk.

"So, does that mean you didn't love me back then?" Disappointment crossed his face, and I laughed.

"All right, whiney baby. I'll tell you," I said, touching a finger to his lips. "I knew I loved you when you spent all day long removing the paint from poor Sparky's coat. But, Benjamin, I love you more now than I did then."

"Sweetheart." He leaned toward me, and I waited expectantly.

A blaze of light interrupted the tender moment, and the front door swung open.

"Oh, sorry, I heard voices." Miss Jane grinned and slammed the door. The light went out.

I felt Benjamin's warm breath on my face, and then his lips found mine in the darkness.

Frances L. Devine spent most of her childhood, teen, and young adult years in Dallas, Texas, but lived for five years in a little country community called Brushy Creek among the beautiful Pine woods of East Texas. There she wrote her first story at the age of nine. She moved to southwest Missouri more than twenty years ago and fell in love with the hills, the fall colors, and Silver Dollar City. Frances has always loved to read, especially mysteries, and considers herself blessed to have the opportunity to write in her favorite genre. She is the mother of seven adult children and has fourteen wonderful grandchildren.

Frances is happy to hear from her fans. E-mail her at fd1140writes@aol.com.

You may correspond with this author by writing:

Franccs Devine
Author Relations
PO Box 721
Uhrichsville, OH 44683

Center Point Publishing
600 Brooks Road • PO Box 1
Thorndike ME 04986-0001 USA

(207) 568-3717

US & Canada:
1 800 929-9108
www.centerpointlargeprint.com